RESCUED HEARTS

Trying to escape their problems,
only leads to more.

An Inspirational Historical Romance
Novel by Award Winning Author

Eva Maria Hamilton

Bible quotes taken from the New King James Version.

Cover Design by Eva Maria Hamilton

This is a work of fiction. Names, characters, places, and incidents, are either the product of the author's imagination or are used fictitiously, and any resemblance to actual persons, living or dead, business establishments, events or locales is entirely coincidental.

ISBN: 978-1-0689907-4-8

http://www.LilacLanePublishing.com

Lilac
Lane
Publishing

Dedicated with love to my family,
especially my husband, Jason;
daughters, Michelina and Angelina;
collies, Daisy and Glory; parents, Bob
and Lina; and brother, Bill.

Thank You, God, for all of my
blessings.

Let us therefore come boldly to the
throne of grace, that we may obtain
mercy and find grace to help in time
of need."
Hebrews 4:16

Newark, Upper Canada

December 1813

During the War of 1812

amilyn West stopped breathing. Her body froze colder than the dawn's winter air that slashed her skin. Never in her twenty-seven years had she come face to face with such a monster. Its large, unfeeling, yellow eyes glared at her, whilst its erect ears dipped down as it hissed. The sound shook her.

Alone with this beast in the wilderness, the sight of its menacing fangs sickened her stomach. She could imagine those teeth dripping with blood after they ripped apart her flesh. Was this how her life would end? Torn apart as she walked to her place of employment, just to satisfy this creature's need for a meal?

God I know better than to attempt to bargain with You. But please, just this once, if You save me, I shall turn over a new leaf. I've been trying—hard—I just need more time.

The creature's paws stomped in a furry of movement as it charged a few feet closer. Its strong, elongated tail whipped furiously behind it and she could no longer think of anything besides its sandy brown, muscular body that stalked her. She didn't even shiver as a frigid cold wind blew and made the killer's whiskers twitch.

She stood stupefied as the animal charged once more with precision to narrow the gap between them. Calmly it watched her, judged her, calculated its next move to determine when it ought to strike to kill.

She swallowed hard, the icy air dried her throat and awoke her senses. No doubt, those paws housed claws just as sharp and long as its fangs. And she kept her eyes glued to the malicious animal as she gradually backed away. She wasn't about to let it overpower her without a struggle.

"Be gone!" She lengthened her body as big as she could to intimidate the beast.

It merely stared.

"I'm not ready to die!" She squatted down, grabbed some rocks, then jumped to her feet and screamed, "Get away with you!" she seethed and kept her mouth open to show the fiend she too had teeth.

"Don't force me to hurt you! Because I shall! I shan't allow you to kill me!" She threw her rocks. One by one they hit the wild creature. It hissed, but didn't retreat.

A cold sweat beaded on her forehead as she dropped to grab more rocks. Frantically, she stood and looked about. She'd be devoid of rocks to hurl at this monster in another round or two. Panic seized her. She couldn't simply run. It would catch her in an instant. Even now, its agile frame could easily leap the ten, or so, feet that separated them. And she was certain it could climb trees. She had nowhere to hide.

She prayed.

Somehow, she must combat this killer.

Cole Munro stared down the barrel of his pistol. His target lay directly in the center of the cougar's chest. If it took one more step toward Jamilyn, that would be its last.

"Away, you nasty animal!" She exploded with another volley of rocks. This time she hit the feline's face.

The animal hissed and shook its head at the pain. Its eyes locked on his. He hoped it knew to retreat before it brought death upon itself.

Unable to see him hidden in the bushes, Jamilyn continued to shriek at her tormentor, "Away with you! Go!" She opened the large haversack she carried across her floor-length cloak and withdrew a dead chicken. She threw it at the wild cat. With a shake of his head he stifled a laugh. Undoubtedly, that smell had induced the cougar to approach her.

He lowered his pistol as the creature caught the poultry in midair, and sinking its teeth into the bird, it bounded away without another look at either of them.

Her shoulders sank and her chest heaved with relief that quickly turned to annoyance. "I hope you enjoy that chicken!" she shouted. "Now the men at the garrison shall miss the special dinner I had planned to cook." Her voice fell to a mutter, "But at least they shall still have someone to cook for them."

She sighed as she pulled her blue woolen hood over her head, picked up her furry muff, and pushed her hands deep into its warmth. Her grey eyes looked toward the sky as she began to walk toward Fort George once more. He knew she had thanked God for saving her life, just as he had done.

But he remained hidden as he followed her. His obscurity was of the utmost importance. And he had succeeded thus far in keeping himself in the shadows. If she knew her father, Pastor West, had secretly sent him here to Newark to watch over her—he grimaced—he didn't wish to know how she'd respond. It wouldn't be pleasant.

Jamilyn stumbled, then chastised herself for her clumsiness. God would welcome her prayers just as well if she looked upon the ground instead of up to Heaven. She prayed, even though her thoughts were a jumbled mess. She still shook from her encounter with that cougar.

And yet, the hint of a smile escaped her lips when she remembered how worried her pa had been about her travelling to her friend, Penelope Sherwood's, home in Upper Canada. He thought she'd be in danger of getting herself killed in this war. However, so far she had never had any trouble on that front. Nay, leave it to her to almost get mauled by a wild animal—an unfortunate circumstance that could have befallen her even at home in the Mohawk Valley of the United States.

But she had learned her lesson. She'd never again carry a dead animal on her person. And yet, she couldn't slow her racing heart. She still wasn't safe. She must get behind the protection of Fort George's barricade and wash her haversack. In all probability, she still smelled delicious to those animals with a taste for blood.

Nervously, she glanced over her shoulder to see if any other wild animals stalked her. Would that cougar return?

A twig snapped.

She swung her body around. Barely breathing, she darted her gaze down the path that cut through the forest.

No movement. She searched the trees. No bodies lay in the branches.

Perhaps she hadn't heard anything and her imagination had merely run rampant. After the encounter she had just experienced, 'twas reasonable that her nerves were fraught. She took a deep breath to calm herself. She could do this. She had come this far.

And yet, she wished to run. *Nay,* she told herself. 'Twas safer to walk. If any vicious animals lurked nearby she mustn't draw attention to herself. And in this weather, she couldn't chance slipping on ice. To break a bone would leave her lame and easy prey for any predator.

And yet, even though she hadn't seen anything, she felt as if something stalked her. She had felt this sensation numerous times since she had come to Upper Canada several months ago. 'Twas eerie. And yet, until today, she had never had any encounters.

Calm yourself, Jamie. Remember what pa taught you from the book of Joshua, 'Have not I commanded thee? Be strong and of a good courage; be not afraid, neither be thou dismayed; for the LORD they God [is] with thee withersoever thou goest.'

Perhaps she should repeat these words several more times, or until she reached her destination, because they had failed to ease her nerves. Her entire body tensed when a flock of sparrows took flight. What had bothered them enough to cause such a hurried evacuation?

Only a fallen branch presented itself. She grabbed it and allowed her seal skin muff to fall over her other arm. "Who's there?" She held the branch out as a weapon.

No sound came over the sparrows' chatter. Had she really expected a wild animal to answer her? She turned and hastened toward the fort. 'Twasn't much farther now.

Make haste! She pushed herself to move faster over the slippery ground. Using the branch to maintain balance, she scampered toward the wooden barricade. The fort's entryway was open and she thanked God she could scurry straight inside.

But before she darted toward the drawbridge, something caught her eye. She glanced behind her and saw a shadow move along the bushes. Something—other than the wind—had indeed caused the undergrowth to sway.

Enough! She spun on her heel. She refused to flee in terror. She had just stood up to that cougar after all. She could do this.

She squared her shoulders. Besides—she smirked—if she screamed a guard at the fort would surely hear her and rush to her aid. Not that she ever wished to rely on someone else. She knew better. She'd handle this herself.

She held out her branch like a fencing sword and charged forward. "Show yourself," she commanded as she stabbed her makeshift sword into the evergreen bushes.

Cole bolted to the right and dodged her stick. But he couldn't abandon his hiding place.

Holding his breath he prayed she'd back away.

"Come—out—this—instance," she

emphasized every word with a slash of her stick through the branches.

He threw his body out of the way, but with her last word, she cornered him and her stick banged into his shoulder. He remained still and it took all of his being to stifle a groan.

She must have felt that she had made contact, because she pushed her stick even farther. It dug into his bone. "You're trapped, now." She stepped around the bush. "Cole?" she gasped. "How came you to be here?"

"Is it not obvious?" He bit the side of his cheek to temper his grin at the sight of her wide grey eyes. "You pinned me to the ground."

Her eyebrows pinched together as she studied him. "Sorry." She pulled her stick away. "Wait, nay." She shook her head and waved the stick around in the air near his chest. "How came you to be in Newark? Better yet, why are you in this bush?"

He pushed her stick to the side as he stood. Then in his most nonchalant manner brushed off any snow and evergreen debris that had settled on his dark grey, woolen greatcoat. "I was merely out for a stroll," he said calmly, even though he felt anything but.

"A stroll?" she scowled. "You expect me to believe you travelled all the way from the Mohawk Valley of the United States to Upper Canada to casually stroll through a region wreaked with war?"

He smirked, "I suppose not." He bent to pick up his rabbit felt top hat.

"Pray tell then, why have you come?" She crossed her arms and looked as if she were a mere moment away from stamping her dainty, leather clad foot.

"You do not actually wish me to answer." *Or, more to the point, I do not wish to answer.*

"I firmly believe I do." Her black half-boot started to beat down some freshly fallen snow.

"But in all probability, my answer shall upset you." He placed his hat atop his head.

"Upset me?" Her hands fisted on her hips. "I was just attacked by a cougar. And then I feared I'd be attacked by another creature—which as it turns out, was you. So please, there's no need to feign chivalry now and attempt to spare my feelings. At present, I'm a wee bit past upset."

"Indeed I've missed your sense of humor," he chuckled to divert her attention away from her initial question. "And how you never abstain from speaking your mind, or for that matter, shying away from anything."

"Cole, if you fail to answer me soon, I doubt you shall appreciate my lack of restraint." He raised his eyebrows in enticement. She poked her stick at him. "Don't tempt me."

"Fine." He raised his gloved hands. "I know when I'm defeated."

"Good. Now explain."

"Aye, ma'am." He winked, playing with her lack of patience. "But first, how about you lay your weapon down."

She looked at the timber in her hand as if she had forgotten she still held it, then let it drop to the ground before she plunged her hand into her brown muff. He picked the stick up and tossed it away from them.

"There, now if I inadvertently upset you, you shall need to find another means of hurting me."

"I shan't harm you," her voice softened. He felt the sting of her words. He knew she had fled here to avoid dealing with the suffering she had caused people back home, and he had never wished to inflict the pain of those memories on her.

"Of course you shan't harm me," he hurried his words, as he readjusted his pistol. "I dare say you're not even armed." His attempt to cause mirth, failed miserably.

"Cole, your stall tactics shan't work on me. Now, answer my question."

"Ah, perhaps you know me too well," he grinned. "But, the hour grows late and you have yet to cook breakfast." He began to walk backwards toward the fort. "I shan't keep you here a moment longer or the men at the garrison shall insist upon my head once their stomachs begin to growl." He turned and walked even faster.

"How came you to know of my work in the kitchen at Fort George?" She caught up to him, and pulled on the

sleeve of his dark grey greatcoat to
stop him.

He glanced down at her. "Why else
would you walk this way with a dead
chicken in your haversack?"

"You witnessed my encounter with
that cougar?" The specks of yellow and
brown in her grey eyes swam with
bewilderment. "And you didn't offer
aid?"

"It appeared as if you had the
situation under control." Her mouth
gaped and he cocked an eyebrow. "Am I
mistaken? Do you concede to needing my
help?"

She shook her head. "I escaped
that beast alive, did I not?"

"Aye, you did." He dipped his
chin. Just as he thought. She had
remained a strong, independent woman
who wouldn't easily admit to needing
anyone. Hence, why he needed more time
to think of how to tell her of his
actual reason for being in Upper
Canada.

"However, you sir, shan't *escape*
this conversation without informing me
of the true reason for your presence

here." She crossed her arms. "Had you been following me?"

"Now, Jamilyn. Why would I follow you about?"

"You cannot answer a question with a question." She shook her head at him, her black hair fighting to free itself from under her hood.

"You're absolutely correct." He tweaked her chin, then began to walk once more, ignoring her exasperation.

"Wait," she spat. "You cannot simply walk into Fort George." Her face pinched together. "If they think you're British, they shall hurt you." Her eyes roamed over the civilian outer clothes he had purchased in town that awarded him the appearance of a British gentleman. "Even if I convince them you're American, they shall enlist you. Then you very well may be killed in battle."

"You'd do that for me?" He ran a knuckle down her cheek, but she batted his hand away.

"Cole Munro, how dare you speak so cavalier about death. You ought to know better," she huffed. "You're incorrigible."

"I shall consider that as a compliment."

"Cole," she choked out his name. "Please refrain from teasing me. I would appreciate your forthrightness."

"Certainly m'lady."

"Cole!"

"Fine. After you finish your day's work, I promise to explain. May I walk you home?"

She dipped her chin.

"Good." He rubbed his gloved fingers along the rim of his hat. Now all he must do is conjure up something to tell her later. He did indeed have the entire day. But even that was not enough time. Especially if he were to remain living as the Christian he had been raised to be. He literally could not tell falsehoods. "But you must promise you shan't allow my explanation to upset you?"

Her eyebrows slammed together. "Pish, it cannot be as bad as all that." He didn't meet her eyes. "I've known you since we were young. I know you've never done, or would ever do, anything as bad as I have." She looked down at the snow and kicked some of it

off the pointy tips of her black half-
boots. "I left because I know everyone
dreads the thought of being near me,
but you, why have you come?"

He swallowed a deep, cold breath
that stung with hypocrisy. If he'd had
his way, he wouldn't be speaking with
her now. Although not for the reason
she'd think. He'd have kept himself in
the shadows, away from everyone that
knew him and his late brother.

But he shan't think of Everett
now. What happened between them must
stay behind in the Mohawk Valley. All
his memories from the past twenty-nine
years must remain in New Callander.
Far away. Some place he'd never visit
again.

"Let's leave the past in the
past." He took hold of her shoulder
and squeezed it.

Her grey eyes locked with his.
"Aye." Did she know how he tortured
himself over his brother's death?
"'Twas a long time ago, and in another
country." She glanced down to hide her
sadness. She must have been thinking
of her own situation. Aye, they were

both here to escape the memories that haunted them.

But therein lied the only similarity of their past sins. "Plenty of people wish for your return home, Jamilyn."

She scoffed, "My pa hardly equates to *plenty*."

He searched her face as he opened his mouth to argue.

"Good morning, Miss West, Mr. Munro," a guard, who walked the perimeter of the fort, interrupted them.

He cleared his throat and stepped back, away from her. "Good morning," they replied.

Her eyes hit his with a questioning glare. "How does Sam know your name?" she hissed. He shrugged, then gave her a wink. She shook her head at him. "For now, I shall allow you to keep your secrets. But to-night I insist upon everything being revealed."

"Duly noted." His grin spread as Sam's approach neared.

"I hope you shall visit me in the kitchen later to warm yourself." She turned to smile at the guard.

"Thank you for the generous invitation." Sam tipped his hat. "My wife was mighty grateful for the extra biscuits you provided me with the other day for our son."

"You need not make mention of that." She rose a shoulder and let the compliment slide away faster than a sleigh over a snowy downhill slope. "'Tis my pleasure to bake those extra treats when I'm able."

Cole stared at her. He had always known the pastor's daughter still possessed an ample amount of good. Perhaps with his help she could make amends with those back home.

He swallowed the envious lump in his throat. His life was forever altered the day his brother died. He couldn't bring Everett back to set things right, but her situation was different. She could change her future. The people she hurt still lived. Reformed, she could return home.

"Life is arduous for adults at this fort, let alone the children," she spoke with oblivion to her good deeds.

"Please, excuse me." He shook Sam's hand. He must live his life in exile, but she need not. And now that she knew of his presence here, there was naught to stop him from helping her.

He glanced back as he walked over the drawbridge that extended over the dry moat and into the fort. He couldn't fix his own life, but he could still enact some good in this world by helping her.

Jamilyn stared at Cole as he walked into Fort George with a confident stride that attested to that fact that he belonged there. Although, she couldn't fathom why.

"Nay, 'tis not easy for children," the guard continued and she tore her eyes away from Cole's impressive stature. "'Tis not easy for any of us." Sam switched his musket to lean upon his other shoulder. "My wife sincerely wishes us back in our own home."

Images of her house flashed through her mind. The ten shuttered windows that spanned three floors and overlooked the front door with its neat little path. The two chimneys that rose up on both sides of the gambrel roof. The tall trees that sheltered the house, which in the summer was surrounded by vegetable gardens and fields of flowers. Aye, she missed her home, especially her pa. But she couldn't return to New Callander. Ever. No one, except her pa, could forgive and forget her misdeeds. Alas, she didn't blame them. She couldn't even forgive herself.

"Inevitably, this war shall end," she attempted to cheer the guard. Although, what her plans for her life consisted of after the war were as clear as a blinding blizzard.

"I pray 'tis sooner than later." He dipped his chin. "By Christmas 'twould certainly please everyone."

Christmas? She pushed her lips up in the corners and forced herself to nod. Christmas was only a mere few weeks away. And it pained her far too deeply to think about her family's most cherished time of the year. Knowing she wouldn't be home for the holidays pierced her heart.

"Remember to come see me later." She stepped toward the wooden palisades, her body chilled to the bone from more than just the winter weather.

"I certainly shall." He returned to march around the outer barricade. "Thank you."

She dipped a curtsey, then hurried inside the fort toward the shelter of the kitchen that lay just across the yard.

*   *   *

Cole leaned against the outer wall of the Fort's small, dark kitchen. The smell of the stew that cooked inside rumbled his stomach, as the heat from the hearth wafted out to warm him. But his body repelled both. He dreaded this conversation with Jamilyn.

He rubbed his eyes. If only she had never discovered him, then he'd still be living amongst people who knew nothing about him or his past.

"Cole, I'm ready," she called from the doorway beside him. His eyes shot open. "They're insisting I leave earlier since the sky is dark by five o'clock now."

After a reluctant nod, he pushed himself away from the wooden wall. Like it or not, she did know of his presence and he couldn't evade her. However, he could always try to maneuver the conversation away from himself. "You must answer one question before we set forth."

"And what pray tell is that?" She fastened her blue, wool cloak.

"Do you possess any dead animals on your person?"

She laughed, and patted her flat haversack. "Nay, I shan't ever carry such an item again."

"Good." His eyes rested on her rosy lips. He had watched her from afar for several months and knew full well her beauty, but standing this close, he could finally admire how

truly lovely her features were. Little
wonder his brother had been
exceedingly smitten with her. She was,
and had always been, undeniably
pretty.

"Shall we." He forced his gaze
away from her and looked past the
white powered ground to the fort's
only exit. Thoughts of her beauty must
be cleared away like the snow. His
brother's death had made certain of
that.

"Did you enjoy a pleasant day?"
He didn't allow his eyes to even
glance at her, and instead waved to
the guard on duty as they walked out
of the fort.

"Aye." She eyed him. "But that is
to be your last question regarding my
work. Why are you in Neward?"

He chuckled. "I dare say there
shan't be any beating around the bush
with you."

"More often than not, nay." She
offered him a saucy smile that widened
his grin. "Only when someone lurks
mysteriously in a bush."

He chuckled. "I cannot fault you
on that." He took a deep breath and

braced himself, because even though he feared her reaction, he knew he couldn't stall much longer. "I'm living at the fort. I've been living in the officer's quarters since July."

"July?" She stopped. "That is precisely when my friend, Penelope, and I swapped houses. She went to New Callander and I came to Newark." He nodded, waiting to see if she had put the pieces of the puzzle together herself. "If you've been here for as long as I have, how come I haven't seen you until today?"

"I believe we ought to continue walking." He looked along the forest path. "It shall be dark soon."

"Of course." She followed beside him, irritation in her voice. "Do I have you to thank for the orders I received that insist I leave earlier to allow me time to arrive home before the veil of night?"

He shrugged.

"Must I pull everything out of you?" she scowled. "I shall have you know, dumb, I am not. I deduced my theory from the fact that you stood waiting outside the kitchen for me at an earlier hour. Hence, you must have known I'd leave before the other cook."

"Dumb, you most certainly are not. Indeed I know for a fact that you have always been quite clever. Hence, I cannot hide and I stand guilty as charged."

She gave him a curt nod. "Thank you."

"For saying you're not dumb or for getting you out of work early?"

"Both." Her steel eyes hit his. "Now stop all this secrecy and tell me what you're doing here."

He pinched his lips together and dipped his chin ever so slightly before he took a deep breath. Might as well just confess. He shivered as he expelled the air from his lungs and made a cloud of smoke. "Your father hired me to watch over you."

"What?" She stopped, but he kept walking. "Wait." She caught up to him. "My pa is paying you to be here?"

"My presence here eases your pa's mind." He glanced at her.

Anger flash across her face. "I came here to rid myself of everyone from the Mohawk Valley. I don't wish to be mean, but I don't want any reminders of my past, and seeing you is one huge reminder." Her eyes grew large. "But my pa knew that, did he not? Hence, why I haven't seen you once in all these months."

"Aye." He grimaced as she grasped the situation. "I'm sorry I scared you earlier. 'Twas never my intention. And now that my secret has been revealed, I shall need to explain myself to your father." He shook his head. "I still know not how you realized I had trailed you today."

"You've been trailing me since July?" she squawked with comprehension. He nodded. "Then I'm not insane with fear. I could sense something wasn't right all these months." She glared at him, her mouth agape. "I cannot believe this."

"Please, don't be mad. Your father is simply worried about you. He's terrified that you're living in a war zone. I do all I can to ease his mind through letters, but he wishes you home."

She looked away. "I cannot simply return home."

"Why ever not?"

"Because of what I did," she murmured.

"To Lachlan and Fiona?"

"Aye." Her arm jerked when he tried to lay his hand upon it.

"I shan't hurt you." He rested his hand on her arm. "I'm here to help you."

"There's no help for me." Her grey eyes grew as cold as a storm cloud.

"You're mistaken. And I shall prove it to you."

"Listen, Cole." She turned so his hand fell from her arm. "I shan't raise a fuss that you're here. If it eases my pa's mind to have you guard me, I shan't send you away and plunge that dear man into more despair than I've already caused him. But you must understand one thing—I don't wish to discuss my doings from the Mohawk Valley."

His lips tightened and he held them firmly shut. As long as she didn't require him to promise never to speak about it, he'd let it go—for now. However, he'd pray that God would somehow show him a way to help her.

"Now please, do tell why you took such work?" She looked him directly in the eye. "Pray tell, why would you leave the comforts of your home to come into a war zone? Your family is rather wealthy, hence I cannot believe you are in need of money."

"Would you believe I'm hopelessly in love with you?"

He cracked what he thought was his most charming smile, but it only made her scowl. "Nay, I would most definitely not believe such nonsense. You have your reasons, and I shall unearth them."

"Nay." His muscles tensed. "You shan't."

"Seems I've touched upon a sore spot."

"If you don't wish me to meddle in your life, Jamilyn. Then please refrain from meddling in mine."

"I see we're at an impasse." She turned away from him, her pert, little nose rose in the air. "Pray tell,

Cole. What exactly has occupied your time since July?"

"I've had the pleasure of following you about everywhere."

"The *pleasure*?" She rolled her eyes. "How is it that you've trailed me for months and I've only now found you out?"

He smirked. "Has it not ever occurred to you that I excel at this job?"

She narrowed her eyes at him. "Your father was a spy in the American Revolutionary War, was he not?"

"Aye." He remembered his pa with pride. "He taught me everything he knew."

"Then he must have been a true proficient."

"Thank you. He most certainly was."

"And yet I must ask, if as you said, you follow me *everywhere*, how do you keep me in sight during the night if you sleep at Fort George whilst I'm at my friend Penelope's family home?"

He paused. "I don't sleep at the fort."

"Then where? Certainly not out in this cold?" she huffed.

"Nay, I don't welcome freezing to death." He exaggerated a full-body shiver. "Penelope's mother was made aware of my circumstances."

"She was?"

"Aye. Your father wrote to Mrs. Sherwood and she provided me with accommodations in her attic. Haven't you ever wondered how the chopped wood comes to be by the hearth with unrelentless punctuality each day?"

She sputtered, "I assumed Violet had hired someone to tend to such things."

"In a way she has," he chuckled. "I do whatever needs doing whilst she allows me the use of her house. Although she's such an amicable, tender-hearted lady I constantly endeavor to do more."

"'Tis kind of you. And she most certainly is." She smiled. "Finally, we agree upon one matter."

"'Twas bound to happen. Even a broken clock is correct twice a day."

"True, and now I understand why you didn't inquire into where I resided." She shook her head, a couple of loose black tendrils flew across her cheek. "I suppose there's no reason for you to continue to be a hermit in the attic any longer though." She tucked the rebellious hair back under her hood.

"That shall be a most welcome change. I ought not to complain, but 'tis a fairly cramped space." He stretched his arms. "However, I must remain in the shadows when house guests are present. My superiors are wrought with trepidation at my having a disastrous encounter with British citizens."

She nodded. "I understand the severity of your predicament, but I don't think you shall be in the shadows much. Violet's adopted children reside in New Callander, and since her husband passed away in May she abstains from entertaining."

His head swam with images of them sitting around the hearth staying warm on the frigid winter nights to come. Nay. He shook sense into his head. 'Twould be better if he kept to the attic. He couldn't allow any feelings for Jamilyn to develop—or more to the point—resurface. He didn't deserve a life of happiness, and especially not one with the lass his brother had been enamored with. He was not about to benefit from his brother's death. Jamilyn was forbidden fruit.

"Mrs. Sherwood, we're home," Jamilyn sang, as she and Cole entered the grand three and a half storey house. "I wonder at her reaction to seeing us together?" Her cheeks flamed. They weren't actually *together*. At least not in the sense her traitorous heart fluttered about.

She hid her reddened face quickly by taking off her haversack and cloak, then hanging them on a peg in the front vestibule. "Violet?" She marched into the drawing room with its celestial blue striped wallpaper atop cream wainscot. "'Tis most odd." Her hands rested on her hips as she examined the golden chaise lounge that lay before the window unoccupied, and all four empty, ebonized, giltwood chairs that rounded the hearth. The large ornate mirror on top of the furnished mantel reflected nothing but light back to them.

"What's odd?" He stood in the doorway.

"She usually sits in here knitting in the late afternoon."

"Perhaps she preferred another room today." He ran his fingers through his light brown hair to fix his Brutus styled waves that had been compressed from his rabbit-felt top hat.

"'Tis most unlike her to change her routine." She stalked out of the room. "Mrs. Sherwood?" she called. No answer came.

"You're worried." He caught up to her in the mahogany library. "If you wish, I shall see if she's in the kitchen whilst you search her bedroom?"

"Thank you." She hurried to the main staircase, grabbed hold of her skirt, and raced up the twelve, straight stairs. Down the corridor laden with heavily gilded frames that lead to the widow's room, she knocked on the door. "Violet?"

A groan came from within. The hairs on the back of her neck stood up. She couldn't bear it if something terrible had befallen Mrs. Sherwood. "I'm coming in." She shirked propriety. If something was amiss, now wasn't the time to fret about proper behavior.

"Violet!" She slapped a hand over her mouth. "What has become of you?"

A pale white face pierced her with moist, red eyes. "Oh, Jamie, dear. Am I ever grateful to see you." She sneezed, then blew her cherry nose into a handkerchief her adopted daughter, Penelope, had embroidered for her.

"I never break my routine," the older woman sniffled. "Never." Her eyes glossed over. "Not even today," she sobbed. "I had gone about my day as usual until my encounter with the cellar. Then I suddenly fell ill." She threw her hands about in the air. "But I suppose 'tis how these things erupt. They take one by surprise."

She fumbled to produce another handkerchief for her bedridden friend. "I'm sorry you feel unwell," she croaked with a shaky hand as she gave the linen to Violet. "You need nourishment. I shall prepare some food and drink for you, and then I shall set off for the doctor straight away. He's certain to know that which will help you."

Because she most assuredly did not. Her specialty lay in cooking, not nursing. She squeezed her hands together to stop them from trembling. The sight of this woman laying ill in bed blasted her mind back to her childhood. Her mother tossing restlessly between stained sheets. Her grief stricken face more wild then ill. The memory caused her to perspire. Her mama's weeping rang in her ears, and her pa's tears made her eyes prick.

"Thank you, dear." Violet blew her nose again. "A cup of your warm tea never hurt anyone."

"And I shall see to a pot of soup for later." She fumbled toward the door. "Are you in need of anything else?"

"Nay," Violet sniveled.

"Well then, just rest until I return."

"I shall try." Her frail, elderly body convulsed in defeat after she had sneezed once more.

She scurried down the wooden stairs. "Cole," she shouted as she ran to the kitchen and ploughed straight through the door—directly into him. "Sorry." She winced, knowing she had knocked the air out of his lungs. "Did I hurt you?"

"I'm fine." He coughed. His blue eyes wandered down to her fingers that lay sprawled over his navy blue tailcoat.

"Sorry." She awkwardly pulled her hand away from the plank of muscle on his chest, then quickly crossed her arms as she took a step back. "I'm glad you're fine, because Violet most certainly is not."

"Pray tell, what has befallen her?" concern replaced the gruffness in his voice.

"She's ill." She busied herself taking a bowl and spoon from the shelves. "She's sneezing, her eyes are red, and her face is utterly ashen."

She grunted as she dug out the heavy pot she wished to use for the soup. But before she could drag it over to the hearth, he took the black, iron cauldron and settled it on the crane that extended over the fire. "Thank you." She bustled about snatching up ingredients. "I shall bring her some tea and start this soup boiling. Can you please grab a couple more logs for the fire?"

"Certainly." He left the room and she wiped her arm across her forehead. Her hands still shook. *Thank you, God, for sending Cole to me. I am glad not to be here alone.*

Images of her baby sister dying moments after her birth flashed through her mind. *You mustn't think about this now, Jamie. Just prepare the tea, and soup, and then fetch the doctor. You can do this.* Her hands continued to shake, but she forced herself to carry on, just as she always had.

Cole dumped his armful of logs on the stone that lay in front of the kitchen hearth, before he shrugged off

his wool greatcoat and loped it over a
chair. Jamilyn stood at the four-
legged, wood table cutting food with
enough strength that the noise from
each cut pierced his ears.

"Thank you," she didn't look up
from her task. Which was just as well,
since he didn't know how she had
managed not to have already chopped
off one of her fingers. Her hands flew
about at an almost unrecognizable
speed. "By the time I finish adding
these ingredients to the cauldron for
the soup, Violet's tea shall be ready,
and then I shall fetch the doctor,"
she rambled.

"You're not venturing out at this
time of night?" He stilled. "'Tis
dark. You may well slip on ice. And
besides 'tis much too cold. Even the
animals have been refused their usual
privileges in this weather."

"I cannot wait 'til morning." She
hit him with a glare. "What if
something were to happen to Violet?
Something I might have prevented?
Penelope trusted me to swap houses
with her, and that included her
watching over my pa and me watching

over her mother. I must do everything possible to help Violet or I'd never be able to forgive myself."

"Fine." He swallowed the lump in his throat. He knew all too well the regret and devastation that came from the inability to forgive himself from someone's death. And he didn't wish that torment on anyone. "I shall accompany you." He made quick work of stacking the pile of logs.

"I realize you're contracted to guard me, but you need not come." Her chopping speed never slowed.

He stood with crossed arms. "I most certainly do." His obstinacy was met with admiration as she continued to work with such a high level of efficiency. No wonder she could feed everyone at Fort George without ever having had one of her meals be late.

"It pains me that I cannot offer to go myself whilst you to stay here." He meandered toward her.

She glanced at him before she started to contract her pile of ingredients to take to the cauldron. "You mustn't allow anyone to see you, correct?"

He nodded and moved in beside her. "Here, allow me." He put his hand over hers and took the knife from her. "If you prepare the tea whilst I do this we shall depart sooner." The soft skin under his rough hand made his words come quicker, "The water in the kettle is boiling."

Beside him, he felt the intensity of her grey eyes. But he didn't meet her gaze. They both remained still. He might not have been able to stop his body from responding to her touch, but he could steel his mind away from any longing thoughts of her.

"Oh," she pulled her hand slowly away. "Thank you." Her hitched voice unsettled him. He had affected her, just as she had affected him. The knowledge shot a thrill through him. A thrill he was utterly ashamed of.

He set his sights on filling up the cauldron. And after a half a dozen trips back and forth across the wide plank floor, his lungs finally expanded with air when she left the room to bring Violet her tea. Closing his eyes, he shook his head. He didn't deserve happiness, and he shouldn't ever seek it, especially not with the lass his late brother wished to be his wife. *God, forgive me for my part in Everett's death.*

His head snapped up. "Violet assured me she'd be fine whilst we fetch the doctor. But I still wish to hurry. I don't relish the thought of leaving her here unattended," she rushed into the kitchen, her tongue faster than even her feet.

He dipped his chin. A house this size usually employed plenty of servants, but due to the war, her husband's recent death, her adopted son being taken as a prisoner of war, and her adopted daughter residing in the Mohawk Valley, he knew Violet was no longer able to keep anyone besides a stable boy, and he came only periodically.

"Then let us not tarry." He threw his greatcoat over his shoulders, as they hurried toward the vestibule to dress. "How far must we walk to this doctor's house?" he asked once they had stepped out and the cold air stung their cheeks.

She shrugged. "Several hours I suppose." She set off down the front pathway.

He stood dumbstruck. *"Several hours?"* He couldn't unknot his eyebrows as he raced to catch up to her.

"Aye." She laughed at him. "But 'tis precisely why we shall ride a horse instead—much quicker."

Her merriment failed to thaw his feet which entrenched themselves in the frozen, snow-covered ground. His mind swirled more haphazardly then snowflakes in a blizzard.

"Cole," her alto released him from his mind's dungeon. "Are you not coming?" He stared at her. Still unable to move. "Cole?" She stomped back closer to him. "Come." She tugged his arm.

He didn't budge. "I cannot ride a horse," his words ventured forth as if someone else spoke.

Her hands hit her hips. "I've seen you ride."

"Aye, but that was a long time ago. I cannot even go near a horse now. Not since my brother—"

A violent shiver rocked Cole's body. He couldn't vocalize what had happened to his brother, Everett.

"Shh, Cole." She rubbed a hand along his arm. "No need

to fret. Stay here and I shall go."
She turned to leave.

He grabbed her arm. "I cannot
allow you to go alone. 'Tis much too
dangerous."

"But someone must." She jerked
her arm.

He held on more firmly. "Then we
both shall go. I cannot be responsible
for another death."

She stopped struggling. "Whose
death are you responsible for?"

"We have not the time for such
discussions." He fisted his hands and
marched through the crunchy snow to
the red stables.

"True. And I for one wish nothing
more than to permanently leave the
past in the past."

He shot her a look. Helping her
make amends would be much more
difficult than he had originally
thought. A deep, mournful breath
prickled cold air down to his lungs.
But he must venture forth.

The smell of the horses assaulted
him, as the sound of their neighing
rattled through his brain. If only he
hadn't agreed to race his brother. He

knew he was the better rider. His brother had never been as adept with horses.

God, I need Your help. I need more strength than I have to mount one of these beasts. Please help me. He walked past the black-haired beauty and stood before a stall that housed a chestnut Canadian Horse. Pastor West had put his trust in him to guard his daughter. He must do this. He gripped the wooden gate as he looked up into the stallion's brown eyes. Mounting that horse was part of his job.

The stallion swung his head high. If it had meant to taunt him, it succeeded. Sweat burst out of his temples. If only his family didn't own a ranch and his brother had never learned to ride a horse bareback.

He glanced at the weathered, brown leather saddle that hung beside him on the wood wall. At least he shan't have to ride bareback, his brother's preferred method. "Real men don't need saddles," his brother's bravado ricocheted between his ears.

"Cole?" He jumped at her soft voice. "I've saddled my horse. Do you need me to saddle yours?" Her eyes held a mixture of concern and pity.

He gritted his teeth and returned his stare to the horse. "Nay, I can do it." The death-grip he clutched the stall with turned his knuckles whiter than the moon.

'Tis merely a horse, he told himself firmly. He had ridden horses since before he could walk. His friends had even bestowed him with the nickname, Centaur, because they attested to his being half horse and never using his own legs, as he always sat atop a horse.

"Cole, I did hear tell what befell your brother." Her warm touch slid over his right hand and his eyes locked with hers. Aye, she had heard the rumors and gossip, but she didn't know what had truly happened. No one did. The only other person who knew the truth was his brother, and he lay dead.

"Cole, your face is as pale as Violet's." Her gaze remained upon him. "'Tis as if you've seen a—"

"Don't say it." He rested a finger upon her lips. "Don't even think it." She nodded. Her eyes grew large. He was certain he could hear the rapid beating of her heart, although it might have been his. "I'm sorry, Jamilyn." He withdrew his hand and rubbed it roughly against the other.

"You need not apologize to me." Her knuckles slid along his cheek, as her smile offered him compassion. His hand shot up to cover hers, then turned it to place a kiss on her palm. Her lips gasped open and he couldn't take his eyes off her rosy mouth. She swallowed, her eyes intent upon him.

"Mrs. Sherwood," her voice broke the silence. "We must fetch the doctor," she sputtered, slowly pulling her hand away.

"Of course." What had he been thinking? She was off bounds, and he was unlovable.

He leaned past her and grabbed the saddle. Her cheeks flamed red as he brushed against her. Apparently, they had both harbored identical thoughts. But it mattered not. He fixed his eyes on the horse, who returned his look with a cold stare that mirrored what he knew to be true in his heart, he could never have love in his life. He didn't deserve it.

Jamilyn folded her hands together in front of her, then snickered at herself. She wasn't a naughty schoolgirl. And yet, somehow being this close to him made her feel just as guilty. He had awakened feelings in her she didn't even know she had possessed. The urge to ward off his fears and calm his soul pulled her to him. She had seen something in him that needed healing and she wanted desperately to mend his wound. *God, help me, I wish to save him from a life of guilt and regret.*

Her heart thudded against her chest as he opened the gate and stepped into the stall. His ability to summon his courage impressed her. And she prayed God would help him. She knew he must suffer and yet he had cast his own agony aside to saddle a horse. And all to guarantee her safety.

She stepped into the stall, nuzzled the horse, and helped him put on the horse's bridle. She now understood exactly why he had travelled here. Just like her, he had run away from his past. And that broke her heart. Her former actions haunted her and held her back from living the life she had always imagined. But Cole Munro was a good man. He didn't deserve to live a life in exile like she did. However, she knew enough about self-reproach to know she must beg God to aid her if she ever hoped to help him. She wouldn't forsake him. And she definitely wouldn't allow him to forsake himself. "I'm sorry you feel pressured to undergo this because of me."

"Please, don't apologize," his words cut through hers sharper than the look he produced. "I may have been taken by surprise, but 'twas only a matter of time before I would have been confronted with riding."

"With your grandparents owning a ranch, I do believe your coming into contact with horses again would be a certainty." She smiled faintly as she gave the horse one final rub down its muzzle. "Are you not supposed to take over your grandparents' ranch?" She stepped out of the stall.

He coughed, and a stone coldness overtook his normally serene sky blue eyes. "I shan't inherit my grandparents' ranch."

"Nay?" she sputtered. "But with your brother no longer here, you're next in line."

"True. But one cannot simply extrapolate that I shall accept my inheritance." He released a sigh. "I have told them as much. They can bequeath the ranch to someone else."

"To one of your cousins?" her words spilled out before she could catch her tongue. "They may be forced to sell the ranch to secure a life for themselves?"

He rubbed his eyes and she wished she hadn't reminded him of the sheer guilt of his decision. "I cannot return to my former life."

"I understand," she resigned. "New Callander may as well be on the other side of the world as far as I'm concerned. I entertain no plans of returning either."

"You shall break your father's heart."

"And you shall break your grandparents' hearts." She lifted her chin and met his gaze straight on.

He grabbed his horse's reigns. "'Tis a stalemate then." He led the animal out of the stall.

"Aye," she mumbled as she retrieved her horse. And her footsteps dragged as if she carried the horse on her back. Outside, she stopped abruptly. Her heavy heart leapt with amazement. He sat astride. She shook her head. He was one remarkable man. In barely no time, he had battled his worst fears and memories.

"Apparently, we're two peas in a pod," he exclaimed after she had ridden to his side.

Hardly. She eyed him, finally able to bite her tongue. He was all goodness. She on the other hand, was beyond redemption.

"Are you certain you're able to proceed?" she asked.

"Only one way to find out." He winked. "You lead. I shall follow."

Cole stayed back and hid in the shadows, as she jumped off her horse and hurried up to the doctor's front door and knocked. Whilst she waited, her feet moved from side to side. Whether from impatience or to resist freezing to death he knew not. Their ride to the doctor's secluded homestead was frightfully cold. But he thanked God they had arrived safely and prayed their journey home would offer the same result.

As the light from a candle approached the front door, a harsh voice shouted from within, "Make yourself known. What is your business here?"

His fingers tensed around his horse's reigns at the man's barbaric tone. He had sworn to remain hidden, but if she encountered any trouble, come what may, he'd protect her.

"Oh," the gruffness in the man's voice changed the moment the door opened and he laid eyes on her. "How may I be of service?" The man looked her over and a grin claimed his cheeks.

His face scrunched in disgust. What reception would she have received had she not been an attractive woman, or worse, if he had knocked on the door?

"You're Doctor Blackstone, correct?" her voice broke as she looked up at the man towering over her with black hair and eyes to match.

"Correct." The doctor held his grin firmly in place. "And who might you be?"

"I'm Jamilyn West." She curtseyed slightly. "I'm staying with Mrs. Sherwood."

"How long have you been staying with her?" He glanced over her entire body once again.

His jaw clenched tighter. For a doctor, this man certainly lacked schooling in gentlemanly behavior.

"Since July." She dug her hands deeper into her muff.

"Pray tell, how came you to be here for such a length of time without us being introduced?" The doctor bent down to her eye level. "Because I'd never forget meeting such a beauty."

"Um, thank you." She took a step back. "I keep extremely busy cooking at Fort George."

"You feed *Americans*?" the doctor's disdain spewed.

"Aye." She squared her shoulders. "I'm from the Mohawk Valley on the United States."

"I see. Well, I'd never hold such a fact against a lady as lovely as yourself." The doctor crossed his arms. "Now, what may I do for you? Miss, is it?"

"Aye." She stomped snow off her boots. "I've come regarding Mrs. Sherwood."

"You must pardon my manners." Dr. Blackstone stepped to the side of his door. "Please, do come in out of the cold so we may converse further in the comfort of my home."

He stopped breathing. The thought of her alone with that man tensed every muscle in his body.

"Thank you, but I fear I cannot waste any more precious time," her words eased air back into his lungs. "Mrs. Sherwood has taken ill, which gravely distresses me. I did hope to persuade you to return with me and examine her. She's such a dear woman and it pains me to see her suffer. I couldn't bear if anything awful happened to her."

"So—" the doctor rubbed his pointy chin "—you've come for my expertise?"

"Aye," she pleaded.

A bitter taste at the doctor's arrogance assaulted Cole's mouth.

"You have come to the best." Dr. Blackstone ran his long, thin fingers through his hair. "Please do step inside whilst I gather my medical equipment. Then we shall ride together posthaste."

"Wonderful." She stepped past the doctor and into his enormous house.

He ground his teeth. He'd wear them down to baby size if she didn't venture forth from that man's house soon.

Relief that Doctor Blackstone had agreed to accompany her to see Violet made Jamilyn breathe easier. "Your home is lovely," she commented as she took in all the expensive furnishings.

"Thank you." He closed his front door and shut out the chilly night air. "Please, do make yourself comfortable. I shall only be a moment." He walked by. But even in his large vestibule he came rather close to touching her and she could only merely nod as she glued herself to the wall.

She was unaccustomed to men behaving in such ways. However, she forced herself to relax. The doctor probably thought nothing of it. He was indeed an attractive man, with his tall stature, dark features and intellect. Most likely he met with women who swooned over him. He certainly fit the description of what most lasses dreamed of. And yet, she hadn't seen a ring on his finger. How had such an eligible bachelor remained single? Surely someone must have set their cap at him.

"I have everything I need." Dr. Blackstone came back holding his medical bag. "Shall we?"

"Please—" she rushed to the door "—I'd appreciate nothing more than to hurry back to tend Mrs. Sherwood."

"Indeed." The doctor donned his outer clothes.

"I'm much obliged for your speed and willingness to assist us."

"As am I." He took her hand and raised it to his lips as his dark eyes met hers. She gasped. "I'm most grateful to have made your acquaintance." He kissed her skin above her knuckles.

She dipped her chin and gently pulled her hand away. She was most definitely not used to such treatment from men. Was such behavior normal?

She stepped outside, thoughts of Cole hit her harder than the cold wind that threatened to give her exposed skin frostbite. He had never encroached upon her as the doctor had. But then, he was a calm, well-balanced man who didn't care for her in such ways. Her father paid him to guard her and she shan't confuse that sense of duty with affection. He didn't harbor romantic feelings for her. Doctor Blackstone on the other hand seemed as if he might be interested in performing both his job and courting her.

Nevertheless, the fact she had even compared Cole's feelings for her against that of the doctor's irritated her. 'Twould never do to begin pining over Cole. He was too good for her. A woman like her, with her past, and her family history, ought never to even dream of an upstanding man like Cole.

She'd only be a disgrace to him. He was better off as he was, not caring for her. And she ought never to let her feelings for him develop any further. She had destroyed everyone she had ever loved and she didn't ever wish to hurt him.

*   *   *

Cole snuck into Violet's house and hid beside the stairs. He strained his ears to listen to the murmured voices, but the task proved impossible. Their words merely muffled themselves into a hum.

But their footsteps he heard as clear as bells. And each step rang as a warning that someone was treading along the upper corridor. He pulled the nob beside him, and before the person came down the stairs, he opened the door, and threw himself into the dark closet under the stairs, careful to leave the door ajar to see out the crack.

A flash of pink calico caught his eye and he reached out and grabbed at the empire waist gown before it darted past him into the kitchen.

"Shh!" He laid his hand over Jamilyn's mouth to stop her shriek from reaching those upstairs. "'Tis just me," he whispered, then pulled his hand away the moment he felt her muscles turn languid. "Sorry." He couldn't see her well enough to know if he had angered her, but as she straightened her dress she produced a huff. He braced for a slap across his face.

"I'm fine," she whispered back, then pushed the door open. "And I understand why you must hide, but Doctor Blackstone's in with Violet now, so please abandon your lair and join me in the kitchen."

He stopped himself from laughing too loudly. "Again, I'm sorry. 'Twasn't my intention to attack you like a lion." She nodded and then hurried toward the kitchen. "I took care of the horses." He followed her. "I doubt the doctor's wise to the stable boy's schedule or lack thereof." She nodded as she rushed about the kitchen preparing tea. "How's Violet?" he kept his voice low, and his ears attuned to any movement from above.

She froze. "I know not. The doctor uttered nothing except a plethora of grunting noises while he examined her."

More boorish behavior, he grimaced. "Don't fret. I'm certain the doctor shall heal whatever ails Violet."

"You possess that much faith in Doctor Blackstone's greatness?" She took a teacup out of a cupboard.

Greatness? "The only faith I have is in God."

"Aye, of course." She set the cup upon a tray and then went to the hearth. "But you do believe the doctor shall be able to help her?" She picked up the kettle.

"'Tis what I've been praying for."

"I, as well." She poured hot water into a teapot. "Everyone applauds Doctor Blackstone as the greatest of doctors."

His hands fisted, but he shook his fingers straight, annoyed at how her comment had irked him. Had the doctor succeeded in gaining her favor?

Of all the women he had ever known, he had expected she'd be able to see past the doctor's façade to the truly withered person within. "You must be careful around, Doctor Blackstone."

Her eyes narrowed at him. "Is such censure your professional advice?"

"'Tis my job to guard you."

"I see." She turned her attention back to her task. Did she think him jealous? He gritted his teeth. "I don't believe I need your protection against a doctor. The man's career is based on helping people, not hurting them."

"Normally, I would agree with such sentiment—" he left his post by the door and approached her at the table "—but before I travelled here, my good friends, Lachlan and Fiona McAllister, provided me with a complete history of everyone they knew in this area, including a rather negative account of Dr. Blackstone. And I believe every word they've told me to be true."

"Is that so?" She dropped a spoon onto the tray with a loud clank. "Then I can only imagine what horrible things you think of me, because I cannot consider either, Lachlan or Fiona, among my friends, and I shudder to think what they'd say about me."

"Pray tell, whose fault is that?" He bit his tongue six words too late.

She sucked in a sharp breath. "I shan't deny the fault lies with me. But I shall demand, that for the remainder of the interval that my pa sees it worthwhile to pay you, there shan't be another discussion like this between us." She lifted the tray and stomped past him.

He raked his fingers through his hair. He had just unintentionally made an adversary of her whilst he had tried to protect her from the real enemy. *God, help me,* were the only words he could utter as he stood with his mouth flapped open like the door she had just barged through.

After she had thumped up the stairs, Jamilyn paused at the top and huffed out a deep breath. She couldn't allow Cole to infuriate her. Violet needed her—and this tea. She pushed herself forward, entered the ill woman's bedroom, and set the tray on an empty bedside table.

With a smile she hoped looked encouraging, she handed Violet her teacup as Doctor Blackstone cleaned up his medical equipment. "I shall return on the morrow to check on you." He closed his bag.

"Thank you, Doctor," Violet said after she had swallowed a mouthful of hot tea.

Jamilyn fussed with plumping up her pillows. "I shall see you out, Doctor."

"I'd welcome that." The doctor dipped his chin.

"Good night, Violet." She patted the blankets atop the woman's legs. "Shout if you require assistance."

"Thank you, dear." Mrs. Sherwood smiled weakly and Jamilyn's face fell as she left the room.

As soon as the doctor closed the bedroom door behind them, she asked, "Be frank with me doctor, how does she fare?" She searched his dark eyes for answers.

"Please, call me, Edgar." He stepped in closer to her. "'Tis only fitting now that we shall be seeing such a substantial amount of each other."

"We shall?" She gripped her hands behind her back. This didn't sound as if it boded well for Violet.

"Aye." He glanced back at Mrs. Sherwood's bedroom. "I shall need to keep a close eye on her." She nodded, unable to descend the stairs. What serious ailment had inflicted itself upon poor Violet? "When shall I expect you to be at home tomorrow?"

"I work from sunup to sundown."

"Then I shall return in the evening." She cocked an eyebrow. "So you shall be present to assist me, if need be," he rushed his words. "And so I may keep you abreast of her condition."

She nodded. For a moment she had been suspicious of Doctor Blackstone's motives—thanks to Cole. But the doctor's arguments appeared completely sensical. "Can you offer me advice on how I may aid in Violet's comfort?"

"For now, rest is of the utmost importance."

"Then that shall be my main undertaking. Thank you, Doctor."

"Edgar."

"Indeed." She pressed her lips up into a smile. "May I offer you some refreshments before you leave, *Edgar*?"

"I'd welcome whatever you have to offer." He dipped his chin. "But I shan't wish to be a burden."

"Nonsense, I'm eternally grateful to you for coming at this hour." She descended the stairs. Midway, she stopped abruptly. She couldn't allow the doctor to see Cole. The doctor almost bumped into her. She held her composure. "Do these irregular hours you keep ever cause you to regret becoming a doctor?" she spoke far too loudly. His hands flinched to cover his ears. But shout she must. Cole needed to hear them if he were to hide in time.

"It bothers me not," Edgar's voice came smooth and soft. She dipped her chin, and turned back to watch her feet lower her down the remaining stairs. "Especially not my excursion to-night."

"Capital," she hollered. Then flinched at the unintended encouragement she had shown him. But 'twas her duty to warn Cole, for she possessed no knowledge of his whereabouts. With a quick prayer, she glanced at the door that lead to the storage area underneath the stairs. The door stood closed. He may be safely within, or perhaps not. She slowed her feet as she led them to the kitchen.

"At the moment, I have no family."

She heard the doctor's words, but couldn't focus on their meaning. "I see," she offered a vague reply, then stepped past the threshold to search the kitchen. No sign of Cole. She breathed easier. But the look on Cole's face, when she had yelled at him earlier, lingered in her mind. She had been too harsh with him. He had touched a wound and she had reacted in pain.

Perhaps he had sent a resignation letter to her pa and now travelled back to the Unites States. Her stomach roiled at the thought. But she steeled her mind. She couldn't begrudge Cole. Home was the best place for him.

"Aye," the doctor continued. "There's no one to pester me if I bother them with my comings and goings."

"You're single?" she asked flippantly.

A sly grin slid up Edgar's cheeks. She spun on her heal and busied herself preparing some soup. She hadn't intended for him to think she was interested in him romantically.

"Aye, I'm unwed. I've never been married." He seated himself at the table. "In fact, I'm the last Blackstone as far as I know. My only

remaining cousin died just this past
fall."

"I'm sorry." She laid a steaming
bowl of soup in front of him.

"Thank you." He placed his hand
over hers. She froze. She didn't wish
him to court her, and yet, she was
unable to pull her hand away whilst he
must be in mourning. She knew full
well the isolation of being alone in
this world.

Cole's teeth clenched so tightly
he was certain his jaw would crack and
he'd reveal his hiding spot to Jamilyn
and the doctor. But they continued to
gaze into each other's eyes, holding
hands at the table. Could she actually
fall in love with Dr. Blackstone?

He fought to remain still on the
other side of the kitchen, under the
burlap he had thrown over himself. She
may have demanded he not talk about
home, but she needed to know what
Lachlan and Fiona had told him about
Dr. Blackstone.

"Such things set one's mind to
thinking." The doctor stirred his

soup, and Jamilyn went to sit across from him and enjoy a cup of tea.

"Pray tell, regarding what?" She blew some steam away.

"Life, and our role here on this earth." She nodded before she raised her teacup to her lips. "I cannot chase away the scripture from Genesis, *And God blessed them, and God said unto them, be fruitful, and multiply, and replenish the earth, and subdue it: and have dominion over the fish of the sea, and over the fowl of the air, and over every living thing that moveth upon the earth.*"

She coughed and a blush rose to her cheeks as she pulled her hand up to cover her mouth. Cole's fists tightened. The nerve of this doctor. His hints at a courtship were as subtle as a skunk's spray.

He eyed the doctor with disdain. The man boasted a reputation for relentlessly pursuing what he wanted without conscience, and if his desire lay in wedding Jamilyn to bear him an heir—nay, he shan't even entertain the thought of such an awful union.

She could never marry the doctor.
'Twas out of the question.

He knew for certain the doctor expected to recreate that last part of scripture, which referred to dominating over every living thing. And he refused to sit by and watch her attach herself to a man who'd lord over her for the rest of her life.

*   *   *

"Good morning." A man's voice greeted Jamilyn as she stepped out of Violet's house on her way to work.

With a hand to her heart, she exclaimed, "Cole, you scared me."

"Sorry." His face was taut as his body emerged from a dark recess in the wall.

"Truly, you must stop sneaking up on me," she huffed a lecture. But truthfully, she was indeed all too glad he hadn't fled the country.

"I cannot—" he fell into step beside her "—'tis my job." He grinned.

"Uh huh." She kept her eyes on the treacherous terrain underfoot. "I lost track of you last night. Where did you take yourself off to?"

"Nowhere. I was nearer than you think." He pulled his hat down farther on his head, probably in an attempt to keep more warmth in. This icy morning air caused her to contemplate why she had not run away to the deep south for warmth.

"How was Violet this morn?" He kept an eye on her.

"Much improved." She couldn't mask her glee. "I think she's on the mend."

"That is wonderful."

"Aye." She sighed with a smile. "I'm extremely thankful to God, because 'twas such a relief to see the color back in her cheeks."

He nodded. "Then, there's no need for the doctor to return to-night."

Her eyes shot sideways. He certainly seemed to nurse a strong dislike for Edgar. Could he be jealous? Her heart raced. But she pinched her fingers inside her muff. She shouldn't be happy if he held amorous feelings for her, she ought to be dismayed, and try to extinguish them—immediately—for everyone's sake. "Seeing as I'm to work all day, 'tis impossible for me to go to Edgar's house and uninvite him. Regardless, I shan't wish to."

"Pray tell, why not?" he spat. "Is his presence pleasing to you?"

"Aye. I believe he may be of benefit to Violet and 'twould comfort me tremendously to hear from a doctor that her health has returned."

"Hmph," he grumbled. But she didn't say another word. Let him think she was in love with Edgar. 'Twould suppress any feelings he may harbor for her.

"Listen, Jamilyn. I know you don't wish to speak about what happened between Lachlan and Fiona and you, but you must hear tell what they told me about Doctor Blackstone."

"I must, must I?"

"Aye," he remained adamant.

She looked ahead at how far they still must walk to Fort George. "Fine."

"I don't speak of Lachlan and Fiona to hurt you," his voice softened. "On the contrary, I believe

this information may be of extreme
benefit to you."

His sincere expression caused her
to utter what was quickly becoming her
most used word, "Fine." For she knew
he wasn't like her, he'd never do
anything as stupid as she had and hurt
someone on purpose.

God, please forgive me. She
squeezed her eyes shut. When she
opened them, they met his, and a
thought hit her. Perhaps God had sent
him here to help her make amends with
her past.

A shiver ripped through her. Nay.
Coming to terms with her earlier life
would be impossible. He may know about
her past digressions with Lachlan and
Fiona, but he knew nothing about her
mother, or her deceased baby sister.
He knew not what truly tormented her.
What memories rendered her dreams
horrific. She shook her head to rid
her mind of the thoughts that plagued
her. They were too much to bear.

Thankfully, he began to speak. A
most welcome distraction. "Fiona was
born in the Mohawk Valley, in
Callander, where we hail from, but

when she lost her entire family to Yellow Fever, she was sent up here to Upper Canada to live with her aunt in Queenston."

She shot him a look. "I know all this, Cole." In fact, she knew all about how Lachlan had loved Fiona from the time they were young.

"What you may not know—" he annoyingly emphasized "—is that Fiona's aunt married Doctor Blackstone's uncle, and according to Fiona, Doctor Blackstone thought he was to inherit his uncle's land. However, he was shocked when their uncle bequeathed the land to Fiona."

"That hardly concludes that Edgar's a monster. Plenty of people would be upset by such events, especially if the land had been promised to him and then secretly taken away."

"But 'twas never promised to him, he merely assumed such since they were blood relatives."

"Ergo he assumed wrong," she replied glibly.

"The problem does not lie there. The problem lies in the actions he undertook to rectify what he considered a slight against him." He grew more heated with every detail he produced.

"And what, pray tell, did the doctor do?" she snickered. "Object to the will?"

"Aye, but not in the legal or humane way you may assume. He blackmailed Fiona for her land and then ran her out of the country."

If he thought he had shocked her, he was mistaken. She kept her voice even, "Let's assume this story is true."

"It most certainly is true." He worked his jaw.

"Fine. But in order for Edgar to have blackmailed Fiona, she must have partook in something terrible for him to use against her."

"She is faultless."

Her ire rose. First Lachlan had fallen in love with Fiona, and now he believed the woman to be a saint, as well.

"Then how did he blackmail her?"

"He concocted a rumor about her virtue, since her homestead had been taken over by American soldiers and she was alone with them overnight."

"That's when she reunited with Lachlan," she mumbled, but didn't feel any pangs of jealousy or regret. She had come to accept that Lachlan and Fiona were meant to be together.

"Aye, Lachlan protected her whilst his regiment was stationed there. And after Lachlan was injured in battle, Fiona rescued him. But his shoulder had been so badly wounded that he lived at death's door. He desperately needed proper medical attention. Hence, to save his life, Fiona asked Doctor Blackstone for help. That's when he blackmailed her to relinquish her homestead to him in exchange for Lachlan's life."

She held in her gasp and composed herself before she spoke, "At least you're finally admitting that Edgar is a skilled surgeon." She smirked. "Perhaps Edgar merely believed it to be a fair trade."

"Fair?"

"Aye. This *is* a war and Edgar and Lachlan *are* on opposite sides."

"You're on opposite sides with Violet and 'tis evident to me that you wish no harm to befall her."

"That is different. She's my dearest friend's mother."

"Oh, please. Do you expect me to believe that you wouldn't help the people of Upper Canada if the need arose?"

"We're not speaking of me." She looked away, a tinge of satisfaction arose from the knowledge that he thought well enough of her to know she'd help people in need, war or no war.

But she must continue to combat any interest he may harbor in her. She must appear rotten, for *his* own good. "Are there any more allegations you wish to spew against Edgar? Because hence far, I fail to see him as the monster you so willingly depict him as."

"Why ever not?" His frustration was most obvious and she bit her cheek. 'Twouldn't do to smile and reveal the game she played at. "If you're correct about the doctor's motives—which I must tell you, I most heartily disagree with—how do you then account for his actions of retracting his promise to keep Lachlan a secret?"

She shrugged. "This is all hearsay. We weren't present. We cannot possibly know the entire story. And you're being completely biased, only listening to Fiona's version of events without allowing Edgar an opportunity to defend himself."

"Jamilyn, the man told everyone she had committed treason. If she had remained in Upper Canada, she would've been sent to trial, and then hung. Is that how a good man behaves? Especially toward his uncle's step-niece?"

"Again, you're judgement is entirely based on Fiona's recollection of events. And besides, did not everything work out for the best? Are not Lachlan and Fiona now blissfully married?"

"That is beside the point."

"Perhaps, but I shall forgo judgment until I myself become better acquainted with Edgar. And thus far, he's exhibited nothing but a desire to offer his aid."

He looked at the nearing fort. "Please, at least promise me you shall take heed of my warning and not allow your guard to drop around that man."

"Duly noted." She waved at the guard on duty. "And you must agree to leave an ounce of room open for Edgar to prove your theory wrong, or if not, to allow for the chance that people can indeed change."

"Fine." He eyed her. "Certainly people can change, but they must desire to do so."

She swallowed hard, knowing full well he now referred to her. It hurt to hide the fact that she had changed from him. But 'twas for his own good. He'd remain uninterested in her if he thought her merciless.

Their boots clanked over the drawbridge and once they had entered the fort she dipped a curtsey, "Until to-night."

He tipped his hat and strode off toward the officers' building. Her eyes lingered on him before she fought her way through the snow to the kitchen. She had been trying her hardest to become the woman her pa wished her to be. The woman she had always thought she'd be. The woman God had called her to be. But 'twas too little too late for her to ever be considered a good wife for a man like Cole.

She sighed. God knew of her struggle to change and she must simply take solace in that.

* * *

In the same way she always had, Jamilyn called out after she had returned from work later that day—only this time, one word was different, "Mrs. Sherwood, we're home."

"Who is *we*?" Violet's melodic voice came from the drawing room.

She blushed. An opportunity had not presented itself for her to tell Violet she knew about Cole. However, she did like the sound of *we*. "I'm most happy to see you in your usual spot knitting." She smiled with appreciation to see her dressed, and in one of her favourite pale lavender gowns, which did indeed bode well.

"How do you feel?" Cole stepped out from behind her.

"Cole!" Violet's eyes darted between them.

"No need to fret." He smiled. "She knows my circumstances and she's accepted them graciously." He glanced at her with a questioning expression. Perhaps he thought that after their heated discussion this morning, and their quiet walk home, she had changed her mind.

"Aye." She went to Violet's side. "If his presence here eases my pa's mind, I shan't send him away." Some emotion, possibly disappointment, flashed across his face. But he couldn't be disappointed she had wished him to stay for her pa's sake and not for her own.

"Splendid." Violet's hand fell to her heart. "And I must apologize to you both for the scare I caused you yesterday. I do feel so much more like myself today. So much so, that I believe Doctor Blackstone need not even come."

She winced. He now had another person to support him on that account. She avoided his eyes. "That is wonderful, Mrs. Sherwood, but I would feel much better if the doctor did examine you one final time."

"Whatever makes you feel better." Violet patted her hand with a wink. *Oh, dear.* She pursed her lips. Violet thought her interested in Edgar romantically, as well. She most definitely did not desire anyone to play matchmaker with her life.

"Please allow me to prepare you tea and then begin supper?" she quickly changed the subject.

"I'd like that very much." Violet turned her grin to Cole. "And you must dine with us from now on."

"Thank you." He dipped his chin. "The company shall be much more preferable." A lump caught in her throat. He had spent his nights alone because of her—because her pa believed she'd be adverse to have him guard her.

She grimaced. She would have detested that much solitude— entirely too much time to think. And her heart went out to him. He probably hadn't relished that much time alone either—too much opportunity to ruminate over his deceased brother.

"I shall make haste." She tucked Violet's blanket around her.

"May I be of any assistance?" he asked.

"Thank you, but nay. Violet must be in want of company and you are sure to delight." She escaped before they could offer any disagreement. He mustn't spend any more time with her than necessary. And yet—she hugged herself—if only she weren't a broken vessel.

Cole sank into the comfort of the embellished, gold chair next to the hearth. The heat from the fire warmed him after his long, chilly walk home with Jamilyn. How nice to sit in the drawing room instead of hiding himself away in dark, cramped crevices.

"I'm relieved to hear that Jamie took the news of you being here so well." Mrs. Sherwood's expert hands didn't cease knitting as she eyed him. "Her father shall be happy to hear of

it. He abhorred keeping that secret
from her."

"Aye," he spoke over the peaceful
rhythm of her clicking needles. "I
shall write to him tomorrow, and I
shall be happy to include the fact
that everyone here is in good health."

"Aye. And I shall never break
from my routine again."

His brows pinched together. "I
hope you don't think me impertinent,
but how did you break from your
routine?"

"Nay, not at all." Her needles
stilled. "I went into the basement.
That is where I stored my husband's
things upon his death. I couldn't bear
to look upon them once he had passed.
But yesterday, I cannot explain why,
but my mind was filled with dread,
thinking of his possessions down there
amongst such must and mold. Oh, the
smell that greeted me when I traversed
the stairs proved my mind hadn't
exaggerated. But I pressed on because
I felt compelled to find the one item
he valued most—his pocket watch." She
pulled it out and showed him. "His
father had presented it to him, and he

was never without it. Now I don't think I shall ever part with it, until of course, I bequeath it to our adopted son, PJ, as my husband would have wished."

He forced a smile. "I'm certain your son shall treasure it as you both have."

Her eyes misted as she turned it over between her fingers. He didn't say more, his thoughts had flown back to his brother. His brother was supposed to have inherited everything, not him.

Carrying a tea tray back to the drawing room, Jamilyn stopped and set it down on a vestibule table when a knock sounded at the front door. "Edgar." She stood motionless in the doorway. "I hadn't expected you this early," she raised her voice, hoping Cole would hear and hide.

"I'm sorry. I thought only to please you with my presence. Did you not wish me to come?"

"Aye." She stepped back. "That is, aye I am most glad you're here.

Please, do come in." She moved to the side to allow him room to enter.

A grin split his face. "Good, because it pleases me greatly to be here with you as well." His gaze remained steadfast as he took off beaver-felt top hat. "You look lovely as always."

"Thank you." She reached for his hat. "Please allow me to hang your things." She spun from his all-encompassing stare to rest his top hat on a shelf, then turned back to take his greatcoat with its lavish capes. She had never entertained a beau, or a proper suitor for that matter, but that didn't equate to her being oblivious to the doctor's attentions. For all intents and purposes, he appeared eager to court her. "I'm preparing soup for supper, would you care to join us?"

"Aye." The doctor straightened his waist coat. "As long as 'tis not an imposition."

"Certainly not." She hung his greatcoat. "'Tis the least we could do." She smiled to hide how nervous she felt about what would happen after she loudly uttered, "Mrs. Sherwood is much recovered today. She's in the drawing room if you wish to examine her before supper." Hopefully Cole was nowhere in sight by now.

"Indeed. But before I visit with her—" his voice dropped to a whisper as he stepped in closer and leaned down "—I've witnessed cases akin to Mrs. Sherwood's, and I must warn you—"

"Warn me?" she croaked, her body rigid. "I believe Mrs. Sherwood is on the mend." The doctor's presence had caused her to fear for Cole, she had never imagined Violet might still be in danger.

The doctor slowly shook his head and looked at her as if she were an unfortunate child who had made a monumental mistake. "She may appear improved, but with cases like hers, I'm afraid it shan't last. She may feel well now, but in my experience, 'tis not likely to persist."

She gasped. "How ill do you suppose she shall become?" She couldn't broach the question that

crashed through her mind—would Mrs.
Sherwood die?
        "Only time shall tell."

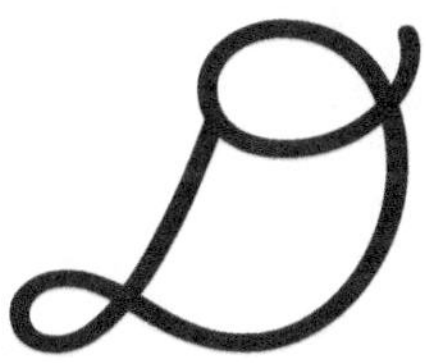

octor Blackstone laid a hand on Jamilyn's shaking shoulder. "I'm sorry to be the bearer of such dreadful tidings, but I always think it befitting to speak truthfully about such matters of life and death. I shan't wish you to be taken unaware if Mrs. Sherwood's health was to drastically worsen."

"Thank you." She could barely form the words, her mind stumbled in a jumbled mess. Mrs. Sherwood may not live to see the new year, or her children again. She must write to Penelope at once. Her friend would most definitely wish to know of her mother's condition. "Is there nothing we can do?" she forced her lips to move, then held her breath for the answer.

He took hold of both her shoulders, his face mere inches from hers. "I assure you, I shall do everything within my power to heal her. And I know this may sound boastful, but you must know, I'm one of, if not the best, doctor in Upper Canada. If anyone can help Mrs. Sherwood, 'tis I."

She nodded. "I would be eternally grateful. I shall pray that God works tirelessly through you."

He squeezed her shoulders, before he released her, and stood upright. "I shall come every night to help," he reassured her, as he grabbed his medical bag from the vestibule table. "And, if we work closely together, we shall be able to cure her."

Relief flooded her at the doctor's optimism. "I shall do my part, whatever I can. Just tell me what needs doing."

The doctor grinned. "I already see our partnership shall be a smooth, welcoming one."

"To be sure." She clasped her hands together in prayer. *God, please help Mrs. Sherwood recover. Jesus, this family has already suffered enough with Mr. Sherwood's recent death and their adopted son being taken as a prison of war, please aid them.*

She took a deep breath to steady herself. She shan't allow Mrs. Sherwood to see panic on her face. "This way, Edgar." She retrieved the tea tray before she led him to the drawing room. "Mrs. Sherwood. The doctor is here to see you," she voiced their entry loudly and darted her gaze about the room. Thankfully, Cole was nowhere to be seen.

"Edgar, so nice of you to come," Mrs. Sherwood exchanged pleasantries with the doctor before she excused herself to the kitchen, feeling terrible that Cole would now spend another night alone.

*   *   *

Cole eyed Jamilyn with concern the next morning when he walked her to work. "Did you succeed in obtaining any sleep last night?"

She covered a yawn and shook her head. "Very little. I instructed Mrs. Sherwood to call for me if she needed anything. But even though she never did, I heard her groan for most of the night. She only fell into a deep sleep just before the sun came up."

"Hopefully she shall meet with a restful day."

"Indeed, I pray she does. I detest leaving her, but I cannot remain at home and allow everyone at the garrison to starve."

"I don't think you need to worry about her. She appeared to be restored to her usual self when I spoke with her before supper last night. Perhaps after laying about the entire day, she was merely uncomfortable abed. Plus, this cold weather did cause an excessive chill in the house."

"I wish 'twere either of those, but alas I must rebut them." She looked grave. "I'm sorry you couldn't dine with us due to Edgar's presence, but I'm most grateful he came. He confided in me that he's witnessed Mrs. Sherwood's condition before and warned me of what is to come."

"And what, pray tell, is that?"

She continued despite the disdain in his voice, "He said he's witnessed others who've suffered with Mrs. Sherwood's condition and even though she may appear to be recovering, she's likely to grow much worse."

"And what exactly did he deem her *condition*?"

"He didn't stipulate an exact name." She narrowed her eyes at him. "You're very hostile toward the doctor."

"I don't believe Mrs. Sherwood is suffering from a *condition* that requires treatment."

Her jaw dropped. "Are you accusing me of lying about her illness?"

"Nay," he rushed to combat her sensitivity to her past behaviour. "I shan't equate your character to that of a liar."

"Good," she huffed, but anger still seethed from her.

"That aside, I don't think Mrs. Sherwood is ill enough to require the doctor to visit her every night."

"Do you now accuse me of exploiting Mrs. Sherwood's *condition* to lure Edgar in for my own selfish needs?"

He smirked at the utterly disgusted look on her face. She truly seemed to harbor no interest in making the doctor her husband. A wonderful sensation swept over him. Quickly, he buried that romantic nonsense. "Actually, I believe it may be the other way around."

"You believe Edgar is effecting an excuse to see Mrs. Sherwood because in actuality he desires an audience with me?" she laughed.

"Aye, and 'tis not a silly notion," he spat. "You are a beautiful woman."

She dabbed at her tears of laughter. "Uh huh."

"You labor hard, you're caring, and intelligent. There is nothing not to love."

Her grey eyes steeled. He swallowed the lump in his throat. He hadn't planned to gush over her. In fact, his declaration had taken him as aback as she looked.

"Anyone acquainted with my past must be mindful that I shall never make a good wife."

"I disagree." He returned her severe look. "I am well aware of your past."

"You're aware of some, but I assure you, you're unfamiliar with the lot." She shook her head, and gazed out into the distance.

"I need not know every aspect, for I'm certain you've changed."

She turned to him in a softened voice, "There are things that cannot be changed. Things that can never be undone."

He stared deep into her grey clouds. She stood correct. He could never go back and alter the events that had led to his brother's death. He couldn't bring his brother back. But she had never killed anyone—had she? "Please tell me to what you are referring." He gently laid his hand on her back. "Perhaps if you confided in someone you'd realize 'tis not as bad as you believe it to be."

"Or, perhaps, I'd realize 'tis far worse, and thus be unable to even continue my endeavor to live as a seemingly normal human being." She turned so his hand fell away from her. "My goal is singular—to survive. And the only way I know how to accomplish that, is to never think of the past."

"You cannot run from it."

"Why ever not?" She glared at him. "You are."

"My approach has yielded no success." He grimaced. "My brother is present in every one of my waking thoughts and every one of my dreams, and the farther I go, and the more time that passes, the stronger the memories. I know not what to do. However, if I continue on as such, I fear for my sanity."

She stopped before they reached the drawbridge. "I understand."

"I knew you would. 'Tis why I believe we must help one another."

"Wait." She took a step back. "I know not if I'm ready, or if I shall ever be ready, for such a task."

"I understand, and I shan't pressure you. Mull it over. I'm not about to go anywhere."

She studied him for a long moment, thoughts must have warred within her. Then a smile split and she cut the tension with a joke, "You may remain here if it pleases you, but I must proceed to work." Had she learned that tactic from him? She sashayed across the drawbridge and into the fort without a backwards glance.

He shook his head with a grin. Procuring her confidence may prove even more of a challenge than inducing a horse to talk. But he would most willingly enter into such a challenge. And he came armed. He knew firsthand what torture chamber she had locked herself away in, because he sat in the cell next to her.

The wind howled with such ferocity on their walk home that Jamilyn and Cole kept their faces covered to fight off the bitter cold. "I cannot wait until spring." She undid her cloak after they had entered Mrs. Sherwood's house.

"Aye." He shrugged off his greatcoat and hung it next to hers. "'Tis chilly in here, do you not think?" He shivered.

"You don't suppose Mrs. Sherwood let the fires go out?" She rubbed her hands together as she set off for the drawing room. "There's no fire."

"Or Mrs. Sherwood." He blew into his hands.

"Oh nay, she's broken her routine." She hastened to the stairs. "Something's amiss."

"Aye, she adores her routine," he mused. "I shall light the fires again."

"Thank you," she called as she bounded up the stairs. He headed for the kitchen. Sure enough the fire in that hearth had died down to barely perceptible red embers, as well.

"I've never witnessed a person suffer such malady," she burst into the kitchen as he placed the final log on the now roaring fire. "She's even more pale than yesterday." She filled Mrs. Sherwood's pitcher with water from the kettle hanging on the hearth's crane.

He carried the heavy pitcher upstairs. "Was she abed the entire day?"

"Aye." She followed him.

"Huh." His thoughts raced to an explanation for Mrs. Sherwood's condition.

"Perhaps now you may begin to believe the doctor?"

"I was certain Mrs. Sherwood's condition was caused by nothing more than the inhalation of too much dust and mold from her excursion into the basement the other day."

Her hands rested on her hips. "There were no such excursions today.

Now, how shall you explain her illness?"

"I know not." His lips tightened. "What symptoms does she exhibit?"

She shook her head. "'Tisn't my intention to insult you, but you're not a doctor."

"Thank you for the clarification." All emotion dropped from his features. "However, as her friend, I do wish to know what ails her so I may offer my assistance."

"Are you certain? 'Tis most unpleasant."

"I shall manage."

She nodded solemnly. "She moaned the entirety of last night. I simply thought she had suffered from terrible dreams. I didn't suspect 'twas due to severe abdominal pain. And today, she's vomited several times, has experienced diarrhea and—" she lowered her voice "—her urine is red."

"Blood?" His eyebrows slammed together. "That doesn't bode well."

"Aye." Her eyes misted. "But I shan't despair, I shall hope the doctor can help."

His mistrust of the doctor sealed his lips shut. Something was amiss. And that man seemed to be at the center of it. Not that he'd voice his opinion whilst she trembled. But he'd most certainly keep a close eye on that doctor. Mrs. Sherwood's health had been improving before that man had visited with her last night.

"Cole, I'm dying," Mrs. Sherwood wailed when they stepped into her leafy green wallpapered room.

He cringed knowing Jamilyn's reaction even before he glanced at her. Terror stricken, her lips were sewn together tight. He set the pitcher on Violet's bedside table. "We shall pray your departure from this world isn't for a good many more years." He took the woman's hand.

She nodded, but then shook her head. "If 'tis God's will, then who am I to argue?"

He patted her hand. He shan't argue with an ill woman either. "Then we shall pray your pain subsides."

"Jesus never complained about his pain." She gripped her stomach and bit back a scream of agony.

Jamilyn ran to her side. "You mustn't fret, Mrs. Sherwood." Her eyes pleaded with him for assistance.

His tongue tied. Everything he uttered seemed to fail at offering comfort. "I hear someone at the door."

"That must be Edgar." Jamilyn shot Violet a smile. "He's come to help. I shall show him in." She strode past him. "Hide," she barked as a second, much louder, knock sounded.

He eyed a spot to hide in the shadows of Mrs. Sherwood's bedroom, but lingered in the hall to listen as she ran down the stairs and flung the front door open. "Oh, Edgar, am I ever glad you've come," she panted.

"Now that is precisely the kind of warm welcome I've longed to hear," the doctor crooned.

He rolled his eyes and imagined she had ignored the doctor's sly look and merely motioned for him to enter. Then, resisted her urge to yank him inside and push him straight up the stairs to heal Mrs. Sherwood.

"Thank you for coming, Edgar," her voice quaked with a hint of—fear? His ire rose. "Mrs. Sherwood has worsened, just as you predicted she would."

"I'm sorry." Dr. Blackstone's boots clanked into the vestibule.

"Please, you needn't offer apologies. You didn't cause her illness." She took his coat and hat to hang them. "Mrs. Sherwood keeps to her room. But after you've finished tending to her, please join me in the kitchen, I shall have supper waiting."

"Thank you." The doctor's feet didn't move. "You take such good care of me."

He bit his cheek to hold in a snicker. She ought to *take care*. The doctor's comment alluded to an intimacy that didn't exist.

"You deserve nothing less given how you've devoted your life to helping people." Her footsteps crossed the floor to the stairs. He didn't hesitate a moment longer.

With a finger over his lips, he entered Mrs. Sherwood's room, and hid behind a painted folding screen in the corner of her room. Violet nodded her acknowledgment, then turned her head away from his hiding place behind the divider where she dressed toward the doctor as he entered.

"Ah, Mrs. Sherwood—" the doctor placed his medical bag on a bedside table and rummaged through it "—Jamilyn has informed me of how unwell you feel."

"I'm much worse than *unwell*." She hugged her blankets. "I believe I shall perish shortly."

"*Perish*?" The doctor clucked his tongue and shook his head with a slight smile. "I assure you, you shan't die any time soon."

His eyebrows slammed together. The man wasn't God. He couldn't offer such prophetic certainty. He hadn't even inquired into Mrs. Sherwood symptoms yet.

"Have you been able to keep anything down today?" the man asked.

She shook her head. "One way or another it all comes out."

The doctor nodded and pulled a bottle of yellowish brown powder out of his medical bag. "I shall administer this. Then, by this time tomorrow when I return, you shall begin to feel much better." He took the pitcher, poured a glass of water, and dumped a bit of the powder in before he stirred it.

She took the glass in shaky hands. "'Tis much less then you administered yesterday."

"Aye, a larger dose isn't needed today." The doctor closed his medical bag.

He chewed the inside of his cheek. It only stood to reason that if Mrs. Sherwood felt worse she ought to require more medication not less.

"Drink." The doctor stood over her and encouraged her until she had swallowed the entire contents of the glass.

"Pooh!" Her face scrunched in disgust. "'Tis bitter."

"Perhaps tomorrow we shall add honey to sweeten the taste." The doctor took the empty glass and set it down on the bedside table. "Now, please, do rest."

She grabbed her stomach. "I shall try."

"Good." The doctor picked up his medical bag, and with a dip of his chin, left the room.

He waited until the doctor's footsteps descended the last stair before he quit his hiding spot. "Do you know what the doctor gave you?" he whispered, as he picked up the glass and examined the residue.

"Nay," she kept her voice low, as well. "I never thought to ask." He smelled the contents, but failed to detect any odor. "You appear concerned."

"I'm sorry. I don't wish to alarm you. But if my suspicions are correct, I believe what the doctor has given you is in actuality causing you to feel ill."

"Yesterday, I did indeed feel better before I drank his medicine." Her eyes grew large. "And whatever ailed me before I saw the doctor just now, is much different from what I'm beginning to suffer now."

He nodded. "May I take this glass to the fort for investigation?"

Her mouth gaped open. "I cannot believe it possible that a doctor would attempt to harm me."

He met her alarmed stare. "Precisely what I wish to determine."

"Why would he desire to harm an old widow like me?" Her hand flew to her chest.

"I know nothing for certain—" he glanced over his shoulder at the open door that led down to where Jamilyn supplied the doctor with supper "—but I have my suspicions."

Jamilyn served Dr. Blackstone a hearty bowl of soup. She merely sat, too upset to even think of food. "In your expert opinion, do you suppose Mrs. Sherwood's illness shall be alleviated by tomorrow?"

"Aye, we ought to see her continue to improve." He slurped the warm broth.

"Then your treatment has worked?" Her stomach unclenched.

"Aye." His spoon hung in midair as his eyes met hers. "But I must continue my visits to ensure her former health is completely restored."

"If you believe that best." She turned away from his stare, and served herself a bowl of soup out of the cauldron. Finally, she could entertain her pang of hunger.

"I do." He stood and pulled out the chair beside him.

"Thank you." She sat.

"Nay, thank you, for all the hospitality you've shown me."

She allowed her lips to slip up into a tiny smile before she peered down into her bowl to avoid his intense look. Had Cole been correct? Did Edgar harbor feelings for her? She shifted her weight on the wooden chair.

"I brought something for you." He dug into his medical bag.

Her eyes shot toward him. "You needn't have," she sputtered.

A slow smile slid across his cheeks as he pulled out a small, blue velvet satchel. "Nay, but I sincerely wished to." His dark eyes held hers. "Please, take this as a gift of thanks, for all these suppers you've spoiled me with."

"There have only been two." Her shoulders rose in protest. "And those were my way of thanking *you*."

"Then this shall give us occasion to be even."

"I fail to see how that is
possible."

"Please." He thrust the satchel
at her. "I shan't be refused."

She stared at the blue velvet
between his fingers. She couldn't
possibly accept this gift. And yet,
his imposing stare worried her lip. A
blatant refusal would certainly anger
him. "You are a most persuasive
gentleman." She opened her palm and he
dropped the satchel into it.

"I hope it pleases you."

She closed her fingers upon it's
smoothness and smiled as he released
her hand. "I'm certain it shall." She
jostled the satchel. If 'twere filled
with coins 'twould hang heavier.

"You appear to enjoy surprises,"
he watched her like an amused fox
might his prey before he pounced.

"I cannot help but guess what's
inside." A metal object must lay
hidden within the cloth. She pulled
the cord and the satchel opened.
"Edgar," she sputtered, as a delicate
necklace dropped into her hand. "'Tis
beautiful." The gold shone and

illuminated a magnificent cross medallion.

"I'm most pleased you like it."

She sat mesmerized. "I love it." She twirled the finery around in her fingers. His grin grew. "But I cannot accept this." She thrust the object toward him.

"Aye, you can." His smile faded. "And you shall." He hurled himself behind her, unclasped the necklace, and held it over her shoulders. She stilled. The man was relentless. Her eyes darted to the door. The thought of running from the room flashed before her. But that would appear most ungrateful, or worse, uncouth. He obviously wasn't accustomed to being refused. She lamented, and pulled her hair to the side to allow his hands to lock the jewelry around her neck. "Your beauty affords even greater brilliance to even the most stunning objects." He stood before her and his eyes fell upon the necklace in appreciation.

"Edgar, the suppers I've fed you certainly don't equate to this fine piece of jewelry."

"You underestimate your cooking skills, and the enjoyment I garner from your company."

Her fingers played with the chain. It pained her to admit it, but Cole had been correct, the doctor did indeed appear to be courting her. "Thank you, Edgar," she murmured. She had never had a man garnish her with this much attention. "But I must insist, this is much too expensive," she found her voice again.

"If the money is of concern to you, please don't allow such unnecessary thoughts. I didn't purchase this necklace, I found it."

"*Found it?*" Her eyebrow raised in question. "I cannot possibly wear someone else's missing cherished possession."

He laughed. "That speaks to the thoughtful woman you are. All the more reason you ought to not only keep this, but why you've also begun to win my affections." She gasped. "I'm sorry, I've embarrassed you." Her hands flew to her cheeks and sure enough they were on fire. She had never had a man exclaim such sentiments. "But allow me to set your mind at ease. I found that necklace under a floor board in the home that belonged to my late uncle, so whomever once owned that necklace is long gone."

She gulped. *A family heirloom?* "Edgar, I'm flattered by your gift, and your declaration. And you are correct in assuming you have caught me by surprise, but since you've been so honest, I feel it only proper that I be as forthcoming." She took a deep breath. "You may deem me presumptuous, hence I shall apologize in advance, but if your intention is to court me, I must confess that whilst Mrs. Sherwood suffers I cannot even entertain the thought."

He dipped his chin. "On the contrary, you are in fact quite perceptive. Those are precisely my intentions. And although I don't relish being set aside whilst Mrs. Sherwood recovers, I do understand."

"Thank you." Her shoulder muscles eased, but only momentarily.

"However, I shall see to it that Mrs. Sherwood recovers soon, then I expect to revisit this discussion once more."

She dipped her chin. He may believe himself a most capable doctor, but only God truly knew the length of Mrs. Sherwood's recovery. And in such a length of time anything could happen. Hence, she had committed to nothing. At least 'tis what she convinced herself of to ease her mind.

*   *   *

Cole poured his hot brew into a mug and breathed in the wakeful aroma of coffee. He had risen early, but Jamilyn had apparently beaten him to start the fire anew. She had even put a pot of water to warm for oatmeal. Hopefully she had slept last night. 'Twould grieve him to witness her slog through another day on little or no sleep.

He ambled over to the table and sat before he took a swig of his coffee. Smooth and warm, it slide down his throat most comforting. He took another long sniff.

"That smells good." Jamilyn smiled as she entered the kitchen in a sea green, polka dot gown.

"It tastes even better." He stood, grateful to see her eyes bright. "May I pour you a cup?"

"Thank you." She continued to the hearth and prepared oatmeal.

They worked side by side, and he had to admit it was—nice. "Do you suppose Mrs. Sherwood would appreciate a cup?" he asked, handing her the cup he had made her.

"Unfortunately, even as good as it is, I'm afraid not. I've already brought her tea." She delicately blew steam away. "And even that, I doubt she shall be able to keep down."

He wiped his brow. "I'm sorry to hear it. I prayed she'd feel better."

"She is feeling a wee bit better." She set her cup on the table, then scooped oatmeal into three bowls. "But even a slight improvement is welcome over how she felt yesterday."

"The doctor did say he had issued her less medicine," he mused, unaware he had verbalized his words.

"How did you become privy to such information?" She nearly dropped a ladle of oatmeal on the floor.

"Because yesterday, during the doctor's visit, I hid in Mrs. Sherwood's room, and overheard."

"You eavesdropped?"

"I was confined without an alternative, and Mrs. Sherwood knew of my presence. But, wait, your question implies you already possessed the knowledge that he had given her less medicine." His eyebrows pinched together. "Are you in the doctor's confidence? Did he entreat you to keep his secret?"

"I'm not harboring anyone's secrets." She continued to scoop the oatmeal. "Edgar never confided in me his plan to issue less medicine to Mrs. Sherwood. He simply stated we ought to see an improvement in her shortly."

"And how pray tell would he possess divine knowledge of that?"

"He's a doctor," she scowled, shaking her head as she ladled out the last of the oatmeal.

"Fair enough." He bit his lip. "But do you suppose him to be a good doctor?"

"Not this again." She placed two bowls of oatmeal on a tray and the third on the table in front of him.

He grimaced. He had upset her. Now he'd be forced to eat alone. May as well finish what he had started then, "I shan't forget that Doctor Blackstone rendered a terrible wrong against Fiona Robertson."

"Nor do I." She stilled. "Do you believe me to be a wicked person, as well?" She crossed her arms.

"I've witnessed you with Mrs. Sherwood and the people at the Fort, you're a generous woman. What transpired between you and Fiona and Lachlan was a—a result of misguided affections."

"*Misguided affections*?" she snorted. "I lied and knowingly attempted to take something for myself that was never mine. That is neither caring nor generous. 'Twas deceitful and selfish."

"You mustn't berate yourself so. You made a mistake. Apologize, atone, be forgiven, and do better."

She shook her head. "Perhaps your logic shall suffice for others, but you never knew my mother. She engaged in the most wicked of behaviours, and, like it or not, I am her daughter. That same evil courses through my blood."

"Nay, 'tis a fallacy. Life doesn't operate as such. You may choose to be whomever you desire. You're not defined by your mother or anyone else. If she chose sin, that was her choice. You need not. And I know you're sorry for what transpired between you and Lachlan and Fiona. 'Tis evident right now through the mist in your eyes." She swatted at her eyes to dry them. "Only God yields the power to judge. We must leave judgement to Him, and fashion our behavior and thoughts the best we can."

"Then why do you sit in judgement of the doctor? If he's made a mistake, does he not deserve another chance?"

He let out a frustrated growl. "Perhaps if he were actually sorry for his actions toward Fiona, but I doubt he is."

"A serious assumption to cast against someone."

"He's never apologized. He's never tried to make amends. What other conclusion could possibly exist?"

"Perhaps Fiona harbors the wrong opinion of him, or perhaps he wishes to change, but has not the knowledge of how."

"Do we still speak of the doctor or has this discussion turned to you?"

She stared at him for a long moment, then whispered, "I need to believe change is possible."

"It is." He stepped closer to her and placed his hands on her shoulders whilst he held her gaze. "You need only look inside yourself for proof that change is possible. You need not use the doctor or any other person as an example. If forgiveness is what you desire, simply apologize and demonstrate that you've changed. Jesus taught us the *Our Father* for a reason. You know the words to the prayer. You must live them as all Christians must. *Forgive us our sins as we forgive those who have trespassed against us.*" Emotions flashed across her face as intense thought overtook her features. Perhaps his counsel had convinced her.

She struggled free from his grip. "I wish 'twere as simple and easy as you profess the matter to be." She played with a chain around her neck.

His eyes fixated on the gold. "I've not seen you wear that particular piece of jewelry before."

Her grey eyes shot to his and her mouth gaped open as she grabbed the cross pendent in her palm. "Edgar presented it to me last night."

His fists clenched. "He's courting you?"

She shook her head. "I refuse to even think of such matters until Mrs. Sherwood is well. And I told him as much."

"Huh." He rubbed his chin, then blurted, "You presented the doctor with a most compelling reason to restore her health."

"Excuse me?"

"If I'm correct, and the doctor issued Mrs. Sherwood medicine to cause her illness so he'd have a legitimate excuse to visit here every night and see you, then your admission shall incite him to stop harming Mrs. Sherwood so he may win your affections sooner."

"Preposterous."

He glared at the chain around her neck. "I think not. Did not you say that his only cousin died recently?"

"I did. But I fail to see how that could be of any significance."

He looked at her flatly and spoke as such, "The man is in want a wife because he desires an heir."

She snickered.

"I'm serious. One look at your beauty would be enough for any man in want of an heir to wish you to mother his children."

She grimaced. "If he, or any man, ever discovered the truth about my mother, they'd never wish me to be the mother of their children."

"I beg to differ. The doctor shan't be deterred by anything. I believe him to be a man who chases what he desires, just as that cougar did—one hundred percent focused on attaining his goal, no matter the consequences. And I shall prove he caused Mrs. Sherwood's illness."

She rolled her eyes. "I cannot imagine how."

"I can. And I shall. Watch me."

"Thank you for squeezing in this appointment with me, Doc," Cole greeted Fort George's surgeon.

"How may I help you?" The surgeon's hands moved rapidly as he wiped one of his instruments clean.

He pulled out Mrs. Sherwood's drinking vessel from the previous evening. "'Tis my hope you shall be able to surmise what medication taints this glass."

The man laid his cloth and instrument down on a table. "To whom does this glass belong?" He took the item and peered inside at the powdery residue.

"Mrs. Sherwood, the lady from Newark, in whose house I live. She received the medicine from her local surgeon, Doctor Edgar Blackstone."

The doctor nodded and lowered his nose into the glass to inhale. "I've heard mention of that surgeon before. I've even witnessed some of his work. He's one of the best I've ever encountered. He can skillfully perform surgeries I have yet to even learn."

He ran a hand over his face. Dr. Blackstone may be an excellent surgeon, but that didn't equate to him being a good man.

"For what illness did he issue this medicine?"

"'Tis complicated." He took a deep breath and then confided in Fort George's surgeon all that had occurred regarding Mrs. Sherwood, from her original basement induced illness, to what ailed her after she had consumed the doctor's medicine.

"You're suspicious of Dr. Blackstone's prescription." The doctor cocked an eyebrow. "Is it possible he mistakenly issued her a larger dose than necessary?"

"Perhaps. Or he may have issued her the wrong medication, because the side-effects she experienced from the basement differed completely from the ones that ailed her after he had issued her that medication."

"I see." The surgeon turned his eyes back on the glass. "Did the doctor add water to a powder?" He nodded. "And did this emit a smell before, because now it possesses no odor?"

He shook his head. "According to Mrs. Sherwood it tasted extremely bitter, and the doctor even suggested that to-night he would add honey to improve the taste."

"So he shall return to-night." Fort George's surgeon rubbed his stubbly chin. "'Twould be most helpful if you could acquire a sample of the powder before he mixes it with water and honey."

He grimaced. "I believe that to be next to impossible."

"You do understand that without the powder in its original state I cannot ascertain for certain what he's issued her?"

"I understand." His shoulders sank. Now, how would he determine what Doctor Blackstone had subjected her to?

"However, I do possess an inkling as to what this may be."

Hope rose in his chest. "Please, do tell," he pleaded.

"Certainly." Fort George's surgeon handed Mrs. Sherwood's glass back to him. "Given Mrs. Sherwood's symptoms, and the appearance, and lack of odor from this powder, I believe 'tis Cascara Sagrada."

"Cascara what?"

"'Tis a Spanish name, but people do call it Chittem or Chitticum Bark. 'Tis used frequently by those Native to the Pacific Coast."

"They purposely cause illness to themselves?"

"Nay." The surgeon chuckled. "'Tis a mere laxative. Although if 'tis improperly prepared, for instance if 'tis not aged for one full year, or if 'tis prescribed to patients in large doses, then it causes violent side-effects, akin to those Mrs. Sherwood has suffered with."

Anger surged through him. He had hoped to be mistaken about Dr. Blackstone, but it appeared more likely than ever that Dr. Blackstone had caused Mrs. Sherwood's suffering just to advance his position and proximity to Jamilyn. *Despicable*. He gritted his teeth.

"Thank you, Doc." He shook hands with the surgeon. "If 'tis merely a laxative he's prescribed her, then I shall ensure she abstains from consuming her dose of *medicine* to-night, and we shall directly witness whether she recovers immediately or not."

"A most risky venture." Fort George's surgeon picked up his cloth and began to wipe another one of his instruments clean. "Because if I'm wrong, and 'tis not Cascara Sagrada, but instead a medicine that Mrs. Sherwood does indeed require, then your plan may regress her healing process, or worse, harm her."

He blew out a breath, burden weighed down his shoulders once more. "I understand the risks, and I shan't do anything without Mrs. Sherwood's consent. However, I must convince her to test my theory. I must determine whether this Dr. Blackstone is fit to be a surgeon."

*   *   *

"Any progress on your plan to uncover the terrible mystery of Doctor Blackstone?" Jamilyn nudged Cole's arm as they walked toward the exit of Fort George on their way home that night.

"Tease me if it awards you happiness, but I believe I shall soon expose him in his deceit."

She grimaced, then uttered, "I'm sorry, my intention wasn't to upset you."

He looked down at her warm grey eyes. "It pains me that you continue to discard my notions, and think Dr. Blackstone is a respectable citizen."

"Cole, he's a highly regarded doctor in Upper Canada."

"I understand he may have fooled many a person. Hence, why I stand even more determined to unmask him. What I propose—"

"A proposal. Why, Cole," she feigned shock as her hand fanned over her forehead as if she were about to faint.

"Oh, please," he chuckled. "You're most certainly not one to faint, Miss West."

Her laughter broke free, "You know me well enough."

"Well enough to know you're mistaken about Dr. Blackstone."

She stuck her index finger in the air. "That has yet to be proven."

"And when I do indeed prove it—" he reached for her finger "—I propose you confide in me about your mother and whatever else torments you."

She pulled her finger out of his grasp and stuck it back in her muff. Her face fell serious. She stared at him a good, long moment. "Needless to say, I'm certain you shan't prove him a monster. Hence, I shall agree. But, only under one condition. You agree that if you're unable to prove your accusations, then you shall confide in me the events that occurred on the day of your brother's death, and why you refuse to inherit your grandparents' ranch."

He met her stare. "We do indeed excel at burrowing to the heart of one another's misery."

She dipped her chin. "Nevertheless, I would appreciate it if you quit this delay. Are we in agreement or not?"

"I most certainly shall agree, because I shall prove the doctor's crooked and 'tis you who shall unburden yourself with a full confession."

"We shall see." She reached out and he shook her hand, losing himself in her steel grey determination.

That is, until a strong wind blew his hat clear off his head. "This weather," he chuckled. "I won't be but a moment." He ran after his rabbit-felt top hat. It skipped off the path between some bushes and dodged him as he trudged through the snow. Thankfully he remained upright over an icy patch. "Got you," he huffed, as he reached down and grabbed the defiant article of clothing.

Shaking off the snow, he turned back to her, but she was alone no longer. A wagon had pulled up beside her and up front sat Dr. Blackstone.

He remained in the shadows and watched as the doctor dropped to the ground to help her into his wagon. Panic seized him. He must arrive at Mrs. Sherwood's home before the doctor. But how? By his calculations, even if he ran, he'd require an intervention from God to arrive first. And so he prayed. He needed to stop Violet from consuming the doctor's medicine.

Jamilyn looked back toward where he hid, he raised his hand in a wave, then took a deep breath and ran as fast as he could on the non-accommodating ground.

*   *   *

Deep within his chest, Cole's heart pounded hard, his lungs screamed for air, but the bitter cold pierced him instead. He had run the entire length of land to Mrs. Sherwood's house, and although his muscles protested, he thanked God he had survived the journey on treacherous wintry ground without injury.

Heaving with exertion, he hid behind a tree and assessed the area. The doctor's wagon rested by the stables, sans his horses. The stable boy had been scheduled to work this day, hence the lad's light shone from the stable doors.

With his sights set on the house, he sidled up to the drawing room window and peeked in. No one milled about in that room. Quietly, he crept to the kitchen window.

"Edgar, I've spoken rather plainly on this before." He peeped through one of the twelve panes to see Jamilyn turn away from Dr. Blackstone. "I cannot possibly think of courtship, or anything else for that matter, until Mrs. Sherwood recovers." She rustled through a kitchen cupboard. "Between work and caring for Mrs. Sherwood, all my faculties are full. And even though I'm ashamed of this, I must admit, that even though I ardently attempt to impart my worries to the Lord, I've largely failed."

"Then perhaps the thing you deny yourself is precisely what you truly need." The doctor's hands seized her shoulders from behind.

His fists tightened.

"Perhaps the beginning of a courtship shall be the perfect distraction." The doctor brushed one of her stray black hairs behind her ear.

He could no longer feel the cold evening air.

She stepped away from the doctor and continued her preparations. "Edgar," she chuckled. "Your persistence has undoubtedly been a trait that has led to your success, but I regret to inform you, that in this instance, where I'm concerned, it shall not advance you." She glanced up at him and returned his stare. "I shall remain adamant about my decision."

"Very well." The doctor dipped his chin. "I see I have met my match in determination. But—" The doctor's lip smirked up in the corner.

She shook her head with a laugh. "But what?"

"Mrs. Sherwood's illness shan't continue much longer."

"Pray tell, how can you speak with such certainty?" Her hands stilled and he knew she thought of his accusations.

Edgar puffed out his chest. "I'm an excellent doctor."

"Of course." Her hands busied themselves again.

"And as Mrs. Sherwood's renowned doctor. I predict she shall be well before Christmas. Hence, why I plan to throw a Christmas ball."

"A ball?"

"Aye. The moment Mrs. Sherwood is well, I shall pour the entirety of my attention on you. And I do so wish to mark the beginning of our courtship with the first dance at my ball. So please, do me the honor of agreeing to attend, and dance with me."

"If Mrs. Sherwood's health is restored by then, the fullness of my gratitude shall be such that I shan't merely attend your ball and save you the first dance, but I shall dance every single dance with you."

He rolled his eyes. The most a lady ought to dance with any one partner was two sets of dances, for a total of four dances. Dancing every dance with the doctor would surely subject them to ridicule.

"That is the best possible answer I could ever have imagined." Doctor Blackstone leaned over and pressed his lips to her cheek. "And with that I shall take my leave of you." The doctor's grin stretched from ear to ear. "I have preparations to begin if I'm to make this ball come to fruition in time. Here is Mrs. Sherwood's medicine for to-night. Merely add it to a cup of warm water and mix in lots of honey. I shall return tomorrow to check on her and of course present you with more details of the ball."

She nodded as she took the glass bottle.

"No need to see me out." The doctor stepped back. "Do go and care for your friend."

"Thank you."

He waited until he heard the front door close before he stepped into the kitchen.

"Oh! Cole." Her face flustered as her hand skipped across her chest. "I am most sorry I abandoned you to walk home alone, but we couldn't allow Edgar to see you."

He removed his greatcoat. "Even if I had stood directly beside you, I doubt the doctor would see me. He only has eyes for you."

"Stop." She picked up the tray destined for Mrs. Sherwood.

"Nay, you must stop." He grabbed hold of the tray and barred her exit.

"Pray tell, what do you mean by this?" She gave the tray a jerk to free it, but he held firm.

"I shan't allow you to administer that *medicine* to Mrs. Sherwood," his voice held as firm as his grip.

"How came you to believe that is your decision?"

"'Tis no more my decision than yours." He held her glare.

"So we're to stand here and argue until night falls?"

"Nay. That shall never do. We obviously hold very different opinions on the matter." She nodded and his knuckles whitened. Had she actually begun to develop feelings for the doctor? Perhaps she wasn't just merely grateful for his medical service. Perhaps she did wish to spend a night twirling in his arms. His stomach roiled.

"Then what do you *propose*?" she asked flatly.

"Let me state my case to Mrs. Sherwood, and then allow her to decide."

She eyed him, then let go of the tray. "Fine, but I too shall state my case."

He dipped his chin, turned, and stalked upstairs. *Jesus, You must somehow intercede on my behalf.*

"Mrs. Sherwood, may we enter?" she asked, as she rapped her knuckles on the door.

"Aye, has evening come already?" Mrs. Sherwood's muffled words shot pain across Jamilyn's face.

He frowned. The doctor hadn't even visited with Mrs. Sherwood. "The dehydration this powder causes must have caused her to sleep away the day. And now, she must be nearing complete exhaustion."

Her mouth opened for rebuttal, but then she darted her glance away and opened the door. "We've brought your medicine," her voice strained to sound cheerful. He swallowed the lump in his throat at the sight of the once vivacious matriarch who now lay withering away under a massive heap of blankets that appeared as if they would consume the shell of a woman she had become.

He placed the tray on a bedside table as she fussed with Mrs. Sherwood. With his hands gripped tightly behind his back, he eased away some of the anger that flooded him. But only a wee bit.

"I dreamt something beautiful last night." Mrs. Sherwood took hold of her hand. "Or perhaps 'twas sometime today." Confusion flashed across her features, but she shook it away, and squeezed her fingers. "I was reunited with my late husband." His teeth gritted. He didn't wish to hear talk of Mrs. Sherwood's death, not when he could do something to prevent it.

"Sounds lovely." She sat on the bed next to Violet.

"I enjoyed it very much." Mrs. Sherwood patted her hand. "But the dream took a bad turn once you and Cole entered it." Her eyes shot to his. But he didn't return her look of apprehension. He'd never put much emphasis on dreams. "Everything caught fire. We were surrounded in flames. And then my husband faded away. I screamed for him to return, but then I awoke."

"Such a terrible dream." She wiped a wet cloth over Mrs. Sherwood's forehead. "I hope you never experience it again. You're already suffering enough."

"Aye." He carried a chair to the other side of the bed and eased himself into it. "If you feel well enough we have something we wish to discuss with you?" He leaned forward and ignored her maddened glare. Whatever she may think, his behavior was not insensitive, he sought only to help.

"You both appear very grave." Mrs. Sherwood looked between them. "Please, don't hesitate any longer in discussing your matter."

He took a deep breath, and with a final glance at her he began, "Jamilyn and I disagree on the matter, so the decision is entirely yours." Mrs. Sherwood nodded and he continued, "As you know, I took your medicine cup with the powdery residue to be examined by the surgeon at Fort George. I also relayed to him your symptoms, and he suggested what this medicine may be."

"Am I to understand, the surgeon at Fort George merely offered a suggestion, not a precise fact?" Jamilyn cut in.

"Correct." He tensed when a victorious smile lifted the corners of her lips. "Hence why I believe we ought to perform an experiment."

Jamilyn crossed her arms, her body as rigid as her words, "What sort of experiment?"

"I wish to take Mrs. Sherwood's medicine to Fort George for inspection. Hence, Mrs. Sherwood shan't be subjected to it, and we may witness whether her symptoms improve, and as I predict, she fully recovers."

"A full recovery after missing only one dose?" Jamilyn scoffed. "Impossible."

He refused to back down. "The surgeon at Fort George suggested that Doctor Blackstone may be administering you Cascara Sagrada."

Mrs. Sherwood gasped.

"Pray tell, what is that?" Jamilyn's eyebrows scrunched together, obviously annoyed she sat alone in her ignorance of that particular medicine.

"Cascara Sagrada—" he explained "—is a laxative, that when

administered erroneously, causes the exact side effects that plague Mrs. Sherwood."

"You truly believe he'd administer such medicine to me?" Violet's face pulled into a look of utter disgust.

He didn't hesitate to nod. "I believe he designed the scheme as an excuse to be in her presence."

Jamilyn reddened under Violet's gawking gaze. "Is this true, Jamie?"

She shrugged. "According to him."

"You deny Doctor Blackstone's interest in courting you?" His eyes fell to the necklace that hugged her delicate skin.

"Nay," she huffed. "He has expressed his desire to court me. But Mrs. Sherwood, I cannot imagine anyone hurting you on my account. I would not have it so. It cannot be so."

"I do not doubt your intentions, my dear." The woman patted her arm. "But does it not stand to reason that if you would not, Doctor Blackstone would not, as well? You are not of one mind or body."

"I suppose your argument is sound." She didn't meet the woman's gaze and looked instead at the flowery wallpaper. "I couldn't bear it if I'm the cause of you suffering this malady." Lightning shot through her cloudy grey eyes before she jumped from the bed and hustled around to the table where the tray he had brought upstairs had been lain. She grabbed the glass with the medicine, poured in honey, and stirred.

"Wait." He rose. "You cannot simply give Mrs. Sherwood that mixture. She has yet to state her decision."

"I agree." Her hands stilled. "Mrs. Sherwood, have you decided on the matter? Shall you forsake this medicine in the hope of improving, even though not consuming this medicine may worsen your condition?"

Violet shifted under the covers, then rested her eyes on him. "Although it pains me not to trust Doctor Blackstone implicitly, I shall not take it. I must determine whether Cole is correct. I must see if I do indeed worsen whilst depriving myself, or if I improve."

She dipped her chin. "I did indeed anticipate your thoughts correctly. Cole has always shown himself to be rather persuasive." She shot him a look. "Hence why I shall add my own twist to his experiment." She gave the honey in the medicine one final stir, then took the spoon out of the drink, and clanked it on the tray, before she raised the glass. "The only way I know how to end this debate once and for all."

"Stop!" he shouted. But she gulped down the contents before he could reach her.

"What have you done, Jamie?" Mrs. Sherwood shrieked. "Who knows how that medicine shall affect you."

"Please, do sit." Cole wrapped an arm around Jamilyn's shoulders and led her to the chair he had just vacated. "Are you altered?" He took the empty glass and laid it on the tray.

"Nay." She rubbed her stomach.

"I hope for your sake that continues, because if you did indeed consume Cascara Sagrada you shall experience hours of torture."

"It shall be worth any suffering I endure," she countered. "We cannot allow this suspicion to linger any longer. If you've determined that Doctor Blackstone is untrustworthy then simply asking him shan't offer any satisfaction. And yet, we must know if he's issued her Casca—" she waved her hand around impatiently "—this experiment hails itself as the quickest way to end this matter."

He blew out a breath. "If you'd have spoken of your plan, I would have consumed that drink myself and spared you."

She looked away. Her countenance creased his brows. Besides her father, he doubted she had ever known a man who had acted with chivalry toward her. Incomprehensible. "Please, excuse me." He lifted the tray. "There is an errand I must see to." He closed upon the door. "I shall return to look in on you both."

"Thank you," Mrs. Sherwood's sincerity shone brightly.

Jamilyn's mouth remained shut. However, her eyes pierced him.

"Can I be of any service to either of you before I go?"

"We shall be fine." Violet smiled reassuringly.

She shook her head.

He dipped his chin, then backed out of the room. She had never been akin to any woman he had ever known. She was indeed audacious. His smirk grew into a full grin. Doctor Blackstone knew not who he had attempted to court, and that caused him a hearty laugh. As smart a surgeon as Doctor Blackstone was touted to be, he doubted very much he could ever handle her as his wife. She'd have him branded before he even said *I do*. She was certainly a woman to be reckoned with.

He set the tray down in the kitchen and shook his head to rid himself of these rampant thoughts. Better set his mind on his next task. It shan't do to allow himself the indulgence of dreaming of a woman he ought not to ever think of in such a way. He must set off to Fort George. Perhaps the cold air would be beneficial and freeze his thoughts.

The guard on duty at Fort George greeted Cole, "You've come awfully late."

"I needed to speak with someone about the cook." A sly smile slid across the guard's face. "Regarding her work here," he countered quickly. "She may be unable to work tomorrow and I've come to secure her a replacement."

"Pray tell, why shan't she be able to work?" Sam teasingly drew out his words. "Never mind," he laughed. "I merely jest. A married man, such as myself, knows not what anyway," he feigned dumbness. "Oh, wait." He held up his hand with a gleam in his eye. "Except, I was once an unmarried man, and I may indeed discern your exact thoughts toward Miss West by the way you regard her."

He remained stoic. He shan't be goaded into revealing his intimate thoughts or feelings—especially since he hadn't even confronted them himself.

"I'm sorry. I do merely jest." The man punched his arm. "I pass the bulk of my time alone here at night in the cold."

"You need not apologize." He huddled farther into his greatcoat. This icy air did render the night most desolate.

The guard let out a longing sigh, "Alas, I am fortunate, there shan't be many more nights such as these to endure."

"Are you to be reassigned elsewhere?" he asked, most thankful for Sam's diversion.

He stared at him. His eyes large with fear as he blurted, "Excuse me, I ought not to have mentioned—please do forget this conversation."

"Pray tell, why?" His eyebrows slammed together. "What secret do you possess, Sam?"

The guard's head shot from side to side. He followed the man's darting gaze. But at this time of night, and in this frigid weather, no one presented themselves. The guard leaned in closer and lowered his voice, "You did not hear this from me, understand?"

He nodded. "I shan't ever reveal my source."

Sam dashed his eyes about once more before he uttered, "This past October, Armstrong told McClure how to defend the fort from the British."

"He's our Secretary of War, I would suppose it his job to communicate such matters to our general."

"Aye. But are you familiar with Willcocks? He created The Company of Canadian Volunteers. He joined us when we captured the area from the British, and was made a Colonel in the U.S. army, even though his actions are considered high treason by the British."

He dipped his chin. He had heard talk of the brutality this turncoat had caused in the region.

"Our general told him that if the British attack and force us to evacuate, he wishes them to set fire to Newark. They believe it shall deny the British shelter and thus weaken them. But a man like Willcocks, his foul reputation proceeds him, and I believe he has an enormous axe to grind. I dread the destruction he may cause."

His body froze. No one was safe where Willcocks was concerned. And a fire of that magnitude would cause immeasurable devastation. With Mrs. Sherwood ill, and Jamilyn possibly ill by now, how would he ensure their safety?

Dear God, please refrain from allowing the British to attack. But if it must be so, please help the people of Newark, because they shall suffer immensely from the loss of their homes, and many shall die without shelter in this ice-cold weather.

"Am I to understand the British are soon expected?" He held his breath in wait of an answer he didn't wish to hear.

The guard's voice returned to his usual pitch, "Aye."

He shut his eyes, as if that would cease the reality of what was to come. "When are they expected?" He forced his eye lids open.

"I know not the particulars." Sam shrugged a shoulder. "Inquire elsewhere, and if you uncover the answer, please do relay that information to me."

"Certainly. And thank you. I appreciate your candor." He slapped the guard on the back in a nonchalant manner to appear as if they had been speaking of nothing more than the weather, as another guard approached. "Give my regards to your family and please do take care."

"You, as well." Sam tipped his hat and marched away.

*   *   *

Jamilyn rolled over in her bed and moaned. She had attempted to contort her body into every imaginable position, but nothing alleviated her pain. *Dear God, please help me.* She threw her blanket off and sat to reach the bowl on her bedside table. Her belly had convulsed and no longer could she stem the violent urge to empty its contents.

"Uh," she groaned and waited for her body to cease its shaking before she poured herself some water and rinsed her mouth. The darkness of night had descended, but she still had yet to close her eyes.

"Jamilyn, may I enter?"

"Nay," she forced the word to croak through her scratchy throat. She couldn't allow Cole to see her in this state. "Go away."

"Not until I've seen for myself how you fare," he called from outside her door. "I promised Mrs. Sherwood I'd tend to you. 'Twas the only way I could convince her to partake in some much needed rest."

"You ought not to have agreed to anything whilst unaware if you'd be able to keep your promise," she retorted. But arguing with him expended more energy than she possessed.

"Be that as it may. What's done is done. And now, I shan't leave until I fulfill my promise."

She threw a towel over her bowl and set it on the floor near her, since most likely she'd need it again. Then she laid down and pulled her blanket up to her chin. "Fine." She plopped her head onto her pillow in defeat. "I'm much too ill to argue with you."

He grimaced as he entered the room. "You appear terrible."

"Why thank you, kind sir," she scoffed.

"You mistake my meaning." He crossed his arms and examined her like a rancher considering the purchase of a horse. "I suppose you shan't deny you've been affected by the medicine Doctor Blackstone intended for Mrs. Sherwood."

"It pains me more to admit it then to actually be this ill, but—" she frowned "—aye, you stand correct. Mrs. Sherwood has attested to improving by the minute, whilst I deteriorate."

"May I be of any help?"

Her eyes locked on his. "Nay. My pa pays for you to guard me, not to be my nursemaid."

"I'm well aware." He stepped farther into the opulent room the family reserved for special guests. The walls and fabric on the bed, chairs, and drapery matched in yellow with red and pink roses swirling between green, leafy vines. "But I ask as your friend."

She bit her lip and blinked as fast as she could to keep her tears at bay. "My friend," she mumbled. "Besides Penelope, I cannot name another, except Lachlan, but—" she glanced away "—we're both well aware of how I muddied those waters."

"Never mind, we shall change that." He smiled. "You've more friends than you know. Let's see." He counted on his fingers. "There's Penelope, *myself*, Mrs. Sherwood, Sam, his wife, their son, the other cook, and everyone else who knows you at Fort George." He threw his hands in the air and she laughed. "There now, much better." His grin widened.

"My smile hardly constitutes a full recompense." She clenched her blanket. "Doctor Blackstone must pay for his ill deeds. He cannot go about playing with people's lives as if he were God."

"Nor can you." He crossed his arms. "The look on your face pleases me not."

"Then refrain from looking at me." She shooed him away with her hand.

"Jamilyn, I know you well. You're hatching a plan." He squared his stance. "And I shan't leave until you promise not to exact revenge on Doctor Blackstone."

"Then you ought to decide upon a comfortable chair, because I shan't promise anything of the sort." She arched a brow.

He let out a slow, frustrated breath as he shook his head. "'Tis not for us to judge or punish. Those are best left to God."

"So you say, but if you truly believed your own words you wouldn't be here."

"I wouldn't?" He looked at her as if she had just neighed like a horse.

"Nay, you'd be back home in the Mohawk Valley, instead of in exile as you punish yourself for your brother's death."

"I'm here to guard you."

She held his stare, disregarding his curt response. "We both know very well 'tis not the only reason you're here."

"Be that as it may, I believe I'm the victor, hence 'tis you who must divulge your inner most thoughts, not I." He pulled a chair up to the canopy bed and sat.

"I did indeed say you ought to settle upon a *comfortable chair*, did I not?"

He nodded with a smile. "You mustn't tell anyone, but at times, I do indeed listen." His joke ought to have caused her mirth, but the mere thought of telling him—telling anyone—about her past rendered every inch of her tense, and she felt the urge to empty her stomach once again.

Please, help me, God. I did indeed foolishly agree to divulge my past if his suspicions about the doctor were confirmed, and I cannot recant now. I have changed. Hence, I shan't break this promise or lie ever again.

"And I shall listen most attentively now, Jamilyn," his words flung her out of her revere. "But please, do rest assured, I shan't repeat a word of this to another living being."

She stilled, unable to move. She knew what she must do, but her lips would not so much as quiver. "Jamilyn." He leaned forward and took her hand. "I don't hold you to our agreement to be cruel. I truly believe speaking about your past shall help."

"Then you ought to join me."

A glint of a smile lit his eyes. "Unfortunately, 'tis too late in the evening. There's only time for you to divulge your memories."

She rolled her eyes. "Indeed you are a master at the art of stalling, and I do bow to your uncanny ability, but one day I shall procure the truth from you. Consider the accomplishment as my life's new goal."

He nodded and a smile creased the corner of his lips. "I shall consider myself sufficiently warned. But I dare say you are now the mistress of procrastination."

"I learnt from the master." She smiled, which astonished her given her ailment and the fact that in a moment she'd expose more of herself than she even attempted in private.

"Thank you." He grinned. "But flattery shan't dissuade me."

"Perhaps 'tis just as well." She sat in bed. "I do for your sake urge you to speak about your brother. Hence, I suppose I must concede that this may be beneficial to me, as well."

"I do so hope it shall." He leaned back, and rested his right ankle on his left knee.

She let out a sigh. "Where shall I begin?"

"Perhaps explain your reasoning for attempting to deliberately destroy Lachlan's relationship with Fiona."

She bowed her head. "You shan't understand unless I confide all." Slowly she raised her head and met his hazel eyes. The green swam with compassion and the brown shined with a tenderness that beseeched her. Peace covered her unease in a blanket of trust. He offered a safety she had never known.

"My pa was born honorable. He answered the call to become a pastor at a young age. Absolutely devoted to God, he wished to live as Jesus did, and exact good in the world. Thus, early in his career he found himself in a town where he attempted to preach to those who frequented and worked in brothels."

She paused to determine whether he had changed his demeanor. He hadn't so much as cringed. That encouraged her to continue. "He met my mother there."

"In town?"

She swallowed the lump in her throat. He knew not the extent of degradation in her family's history. Perhaps she ought not continue. He may view her differently. He may be appalled. Her head spun. Nay. She must confide in him. The whole truth. "My mother was one of the prostitutes."

His eyes widened, but returned to their usual size so quickly she sat unsure if he had been affected or if she had imagined his reaction. "Please, continue." He moved so his feet were both firmly on the ground. Then he leaned forward and pressed his hands together in a manner that begged her to tell him more.

"My mother suffered an abusive upbringing and she knew no other way than prostitution to keep herself alive. Then she met my pa."

"And they fell in love and married?"

"Aye. She abandoned her former life, and soon after, they welcomed me into the world. In the eyes of my eight year old self, all was perfect."

"Then?"

"My parents said I was to expect a baby brother or sister. They appeared thrilled, as was I."

"I thought you an only child."

"My mother kept every pregnancy a secret." Her eyes misted. "She miscarried every baby, except myself and my little sister. But my sister—she never uttered a single sound."

He reached out and put his hand over hers. "I'm sorry."

"I can still see my mother lying on that blood soaked bed with my sister's lifeless body in her arms. I had crept into the room, but when I gasped, she yelled for me to leave."

"And then she died?"

She shook her head. "She died many years later. However, the good part of her died that day along with my sister. She blamed God for taking her babies. She was certain God had taken them to punish her for her sins. My pa tried in vain to convince her otherwise, but his every attempt was met with more rage. She spat her hatred of being a pastor's wife. She despised the pretense she had felt to appear perfect. My sister must have been the final straw, because as soon as she could, my mother left us. She returned to her former life."

He squeezed her hand and a tear fell from her eye. "I fear we have yet to reach the end of the story?"

She sobbed a gulp. "My pa attempted to reconcile himself with her. In his eyes, marriage is forever. But my mother refused his every attempt. She even refused to see me. We lived as such for five years. I was ostracized at school. No child wished to befriend a prostitute's daughter, or perhaps their parents forbade it." She shrugged. "Little did I know that being alone far exceeded the alternative."

His face contorted into one of sheer concern. "Pray tell, I fail to understand."

She took another deep breath. "Once the boys learned of my mother, they treated me as if I were my mother." His eyes shut tight and she spared him the detrimental details. She didn't wish to relive them anyway. "When my pa learned of my situation, he moved us to the Mohawk Valley where no one knew us."

His eyes found hers. "He dearly loves you."

She squeezed his hand back. "My pa never forsook my mother though. He was devastated when she died a few years later, and unburdened himself to Lachlan's parents, whom he had become good friends with. They alone are the one family in the Mohawk Valley that knows of our past."

"I cannot fathom they'd tell Lachlan, he would have been rather young."

"True. They did not. However, he accidentally overheard. I came upon him whilst he did, but he promised to keep our secret. You may imagine the extent to which I mistrusted him. The boys I had known hadn't been trustworthy. In fact, I cannot credit them with any good qualities."

"But Lachlan never broke your trust. Blair and myself are his closest friends and he never said a word to us."

"I know. He's kept our secret all these years. Hence, why I believed he ought to be my husband. I thought he had remained silent to protect me, to protect our future. I thought he loved me."

"He loved you as a friend."

"I arrived at that knowledge far too late. To me, he had been the only boy who had ever treated me well. The only one who had known of my past and still respected me and cared for me. Can you not understand? I couldn't fathom ever confiding in another man, and especially have that man accept me as he so easily did. Hence, why I grew so desperate not to lose him."

"Do you not realize you never allowed anyone else the opportunity to disprove your theory?"

She grew quiet as she stared at him. Had she heard the ire in his voice correctly? Had he wished to exhibit his loyalty? It mattered not. She shan't ever grant him the opportunity.

I'm sorry, God. I do endeavor to change, but as of yet, I believe I've failed, and now, I must seek revenge on Edgar. That man must atone for his ill deeds.

"Jamilyn, the look upon your face causes me concern." He pulled his hand away. "Pray tell me your thoughts."

She looked down at her blanket and played with its woolen fibers. She'd never tell him her plans to avenge Mrs. Sherwood's suffering. He would severely disapprove. "I'm rather tired, and I believe sleep may help ward off this medicine more hastily." She yawned, exaggerating her fatigue, knowing he would not protest her desire to better her health.

Only she knew that she needed her strength for other reasons. Tomorrow morning she'd disgrace Edgar, and nothing, or no one, would stand in her way.

He nodded. "I understand. I'm sorry I impelled you to remain cognizant this long." He sat forward and placed his palms on his knees to rise. But she reached out and put her hand over his.

"Please, I entreat you not to apologize. This conversation has endeared itself to me more than you may realize."

"How so?" He took her hand into his.

"You sir, are the first person I've ever confided in regarding my past. And I know I shan't ever suffer a moment of regret on this account."

"Good." He kissed her hand. "I shall forever lament your past misfortunes, but I'm glad you now realize that, besides your father and Lachlan, plenty of men shan't cast stones at you for your mother's actions."

Tears welled in her eyes. If only his words were true, but she knew herself. And she knew her plans for Edgar. She was more akin to her mother than he knew. And tomorrow, Edgar would be on the receiving end of her fury.

*　　*　　*

Cole bolted out of bed. The darkness of morning surrounded him and mirrored his thoughts. Last night when he had left Jamilyn he had heard her vomit as he shut the door. His hand had clutched the doorknob and strangled the metal as if 'twere Dr. Blackstone's neck.

Giving his head a shake, he took a deep breath. *God, I'm sorry. Please help me maintain control.* He dressed, then stretched to release his frustration. But his anger failed to wane.

He rushed downstairs, threw on his greatcoat and grabbed his hat before he stomped out into the cold air. The frigid temperature failed to squelch his boiling temper.

Perhaps a ride to Fort George would smother the flames. Forget daylight, his fury would never allow him to wait until the sun came up. He stomped to his horse, angry at the doctor, and himself. He squeezed his horse's reins as they trudged through the snow. He had letdown too many people, and the list continued to grow—his brother, his grandparents, Mrs. Sherwood, and now Jamilyn. Unacceptable.

The wind slapped his face, like lashes from a whip, as he approached the American stronghold. His list stopped now. Henceforth, he'd keep

Mrs. Sherwood and Jamilyn safe. *God, I shan't allow this war to touch them. Please help me ascertain more information about the advancing British troops.* An eerie shiver ran up his spine at the sight of too much light and noise surging from the fort. *God, please let it not be too late.*

He jumped off his horse, tied him to a tree outside the palisade, then trotted into the fort. He had never witnessed the fort in such a state of upheaval. At this time of day, most of the inhabitants ought to have been abed, instead, it appeared as if every soldier, officer, and their families were out of doors.

"Why such commotion?" he shouted at a passing soldier.

"The British are coming," the soldier's teeth chattered behind purple lips as he hastened away.

He trudged through the snow in search of answers. "How close are the British?" he called to another soldier who merely shrugged as he ran past him. He hurried to catch up to an officer. "Have orders been declared?"

The officer nodded. "We're to evacuate."

His jaw dropped. If the British reclaimed their land, he'd be forced to protect Jamilyn behind enemy lines. "Surely we've not been commanded to simply allow the British back in without a fight?"

The officer threw his musket over his shoulder. "Nay." His heart stopped. He knew the officer's next words. "We're to burn Newark to the ground as we depart."

Newark, Mrs. Sherwood's home. *Please, God, help us all.* The rest of his body froze, like the corpses of the citizens of Upper Canada who'd perish from either the fire or being turned out into this glacial snow. "When is everyone to leave?"

"As soon as the fort can be evacuated." The officer looked up at the waning moon. Panic seized him. He prayed for enough time to ride back to Jamilyn and Mrs. Sherwood before this atrocity occurred. But even then, how would he secure their safety? The women may be too weak or ill. "The Canadian Volunteers and US Militiamen are already gathering. They mean to set out to warn people of the impending fires as soon as the sun rises."

"I pray to God they do indeed have the allotted time."

"I do, as well. But as a member of the Rearguard, I shall be the last to leave, and I honestly know not how long we shall remain on this side of the river to allow the others time to warn everyone."

Such atrocity. "Thank you for your candor. Do take care." He dipped his chin, then trekked as quick as possible through the snow to untie his horse before he mounted the animal and clucked his tongue to set off.

Images of Jamilyn and Mrs. Sherwood standing outside in their nightclothes watching the grand house burn to the ground filled him with panic. He kicked his boots into the horse's flanks. He must make haste.

Please, God, permit us not to become stuck in this snow. Grant this horse the speed and skill it needs to travel back to Jamilyn and Mrs. Sherwood in time.

The horse bolted ahead and raced faster than it ought in this inclement weather, but he spurred it on. His greatcoat flapped madly about him and sent the icy squalls deep into his bones. He could barely keep his eyes open past a slit, as his horse's hooves pounded into the snow, and sent white spray into the darkness as if to expel the night.

His heart beat faster than the horse's rapid pace as they raced against time. Finally, the three and a half storey home came into view. Its grandeur loomed from its position atop a winding lane. To think of all the loving homes, such as this, about to be lost to fire sickened his stomach.

In front of the stable, he jumped off his horse. His head jerked to the east and he grimaced at the advancing daylight. No time remained. He shut the horse in the stable and dashed into the house. "Jamilyn," he called. "Mrs. Sherwood!" He bolted up the stairs, well aware that at this early hour they'd still be abed.

"Cole?" Mrs. Sherwood's bedroom door flew open as she stepped into the corridor hugging herself into a shawl. "Whatever is the matter?"

He pounded on Jamilyn's door. "Jamilyn!" he shouted. "Why does she not answer?" Panic seized him. Had the doctor's dose been lethal?

"Step aside." Mrs. Sherwood bustled forth with the determination he hadn't seen her exhibit since before she had been subjected to Dr. Blackstone's care. "Jamilyn, 'tis Mrs. Sherwood, I'm sorry, but I must enter."

"Mrs. Sherwood barged into Jamilyn's bedroom. "'Tis empty."

"What?"

He strode into the room, unable to comprehend the widow's words. Only flowers peered back at him. "She must be here somewhere." He rushed from the room. "Jamilyn." he shouted as he ran through the upstairs, then down to the main floor, and into every room before he tore open the basement door and continued his rampage.

"She's left the house," Mrs. Sherwood called from the front entrance vestibule. "Her coat and boots are gone."

"Nay, she cannot be missing. We must find her," he spoke his thoughts aloud.

"Perhaps she decided to walk to the fort early this morning. She's done so before."

"Not possible." He raked his fingers through his hair. "I've just come from there, along her route, and I saw not one person." Fear gripped his chest. Perhaps she had encountered another wild animal. *Nay*. He stroked his jaw. He hadn't seen any blood on the snow.

"Perhaps she's gone into town for something then." Mrs. Sherwood pulled her shawl more tightly around her. "Her father may have sent you here to protect her, but she's not a meek lass. Don't fret, she shall return safely before long."

"You don't understand." He worked his jaw. "The British are coming to reclaim this part of Upper Canada."

She gasped. "We're to fight another battle on our doorstep." Her face blanched.

"Nay." He took hold of her arm to catch her if she fainted. "We're retreating."

A smile split her face. "The war is over?"

"I fear not." He shook his head. "Indeed this shall mark yet another tragic day in this war as we burn the town of Newark and Fort George before we leave British soil." Her weight fell on him. "Mrs. Sherwood, please, sit here." He eased her into a chair.

"My house," she mumbled as tears rolled down her cheeks.

He pulled out his handkerchief and offered it to her. His heart ached for her. She carried the pain from everyone she had lost, and now this. "I'm sorry. If I could stop this, please know I would."

"I know." She patted his hand. "But what are we to do?"

"Pray we survive and your house is spared."

She huffed. "If they burn down my house, I hope they're prepared to burn me, as well, because I shan't leave."

Oh, dear. He took a deep breath. She did truly adore routine and was firmly planted in her ways. "I must away to find Jamilyn. But I cannot, until I'm assured of your safety." She sniffled and looked about her home as he continued, "You must dress in your warmest clothes. Collect any valuables you can carry, and at the first sign of trouble, leave your house and seek shelter in the root cellar."

"I shan't leave."

"Your root cellar is built of stone. It shan't burn. It shall offer you shelter from the freezing snow and wind." She jutted her chin into the air and pretended not to hear.

He raked his fingers through his hair, frustration mounting within. "Please attempt to at least remain hidden and I shall return as soon as I locate Jamilyn." Perhaps she could convince Mrs. Sherwood to seek safety. He certainly had failed. *God, please be with her.*

"I shall return shortly. Please, do heed my warning." She glanced at him and he took that as her assurance before he strode to the front entrance, dressed, then stepped out into the blustery snow.

For months he had guarded Jamilyn, and never once, had he allowed her out of his sight. Now, today of all days, she was missing. He hit his hat onto his head harder than necessary and glanced about. If she had left footprints, the newly fallen snow covered their existence. He was bereft to even see his own footprints as he tramped to the stable.

With much effort against the wind, he threw the stable door open. The horses neighed their protest. But given the alternative of being burned to death, he set about opening their stalls if the need arose for them to escape. "There, last one." But it ought not to have been. One of the horses was missing. Hence, wherever

Jamilyn had gone, she had travelled on horseback.

He saddled a strong male quarter horse whilst he ran through a list of places she may be—general store, butcher, druggist—their conversation from last night jumped into his thoughts. He could hear her voice, *Doctor Blackstone must pay for his ill deeds.*

He mounted the horse and set off for the doctor's homestead. Daylight broke. A moment of panic seized him. Time had run out. The Canadian Volunteers and US Militiamen would attempt to warn people, but the fires would begin soon.

He urged his horse to move faster. The doctor lived close to Fort George, hence his house may well be one of the first homes set ablaze. His jaw clenched. She could be terribly hurt.

His eyes wandered to the approaching horizon. *God, please lead me to Dr. Blackstone's home. Help me retrace the path I travelled with Jamilyn on that cold, dark night.*

He shivered as images of his brother and why he had been terrified to mount a horse flew back into his mind. *Not now.* He kicked his horse's flanks. He mustn't skirt his duty. He had ridden a horse that night to assure her safety, and now he must fight these qualms to do so again.

His breath caught in his lungs at the sight of a militiaman heading up a path to someone's home. The eleventh hour was upon them. The plans he had heard talk of at the fort had come to fruition. And he was powerless to stop them.

He pushed his horse faster. He may not be able to stop his fellow Americans, but he would do everything, and anything, in his power to protect Jamilyn and Mrs. Sherwood. *God, please help me keep them safe and protect the citizens of Upper Canada.*

He pulled up on the reins. The trees that covered this bit of path had blocked out the wind and snow, and he saw hoof prints. He followed the prints, praying they were recent, and they'd lead him to Jamilyn before she unleashed her wrath upon Dr. Blackstone in a manner she may regret.

The prints stopped. He slowed, as if in a barren desert of snow. Which way? He darted his gaze about until he spotted a snow drift to his right with a large welt upon it. Had she been thrown by her horse? He turned his horse to examine the ground. He had missed this before, but the horse's hoof prints had changed course and went into the woods, whilst a few footprints led away from the welt in the snow.

He spurred his horse on again. She was not one to quit. She may have attempted to travel to the doctor on foot. But, poor lass, her feet and legs would surely freeze from thrashing through snow two or three feet deep—deeper still where the wind blew it into banks. Nevertheless, he thanked God, this may provide him with a better chance of catching up to her.

His horse stumbled. He couldn't fathom how she had fared if she had come this way. She had been immensely ill last night and hadn't had time to recoup her strength. He shuddered, as his horse trotted on. If she had fallen, her body may now lie lifeless under a mound of snow. He couldn't possibly rid snow from the entire expanse of land to find her. He shook his head. He must believe she had reached the doctor's homestead. But that thought failed to calm his nerves. Her actions would be just as terrifying.

Snowflakes clung to every inch of him, and blocked his view as he pressed his horse on. The snow had increased in its intensity. This was a storm to remain indoors. Not even animals ought to be permitted to stray out of doors. His fingers clenched around the reins, possibly frozen in place, but he mustn't relent until he arrived at the doctor's homestead.

"Jamilyn?" He strode toward a figure that ploughed through the snow. "Jamilyn," he shouted louder. The figure didn't stop or respond. Perhaps 'twas not her. "Wait," he yelled and jumped off his horse. His feet sank into a white cushion that covered him up to his thighs. "Stop!" He hurdled himself through the snow drift.

"Cole?" She faced him, her lips purple, and her cheeks and nose red from the cold. "Pray tell, why—"

"There's no time." He grabbed her arm, ready to help her onto his horse.

"Unhand me." She shrugged out of his grasp.

He stepped in closer. "I shan't allow you to regret attacking the doctor."

She huffed, releasing a puff of hot air. "You assume I shall regret my actions."

"Aye. You erroneously think you're akin to your mother. You wish people to believe you're strong and unfeeling, but I know differently."

"You do, do you?" She jutted her chin into the air. "I'm sorry to be the bearer of bad news, but you're wrong." She stepped forward and her boot sank deep into the snow and out of sight.

"Be that as it may, I still cannot allow you to proceed with whatever plan you've concocted." He grabbed her elbow. Her eyes hit his. "Please, heed me. 'Tis no longer safe for us here."

"Nay, it most certainly is not." She pulled her arm, but he increased his grip and held her tighter. "Nor is it safe for anyone with Dr. Blackstone doing whatever he pleases."

"You misunderstand me. The British are coming and the Americans at Fort George have vowed to burn Newark and the fort as they retreat to the United States."

"What?" Her jaw dropped, and her resistance waned. "When?"

"Now." Sun had indeed lightened the sky and he glanced around for signs of smoke. "The Militiamen and Canadian Volunteers are warning British citizens. Hopefully some lives shall be spared. But to be put out into this snow storm, and have their homes set afire, the damage shall be immeasurable."

"Mrs. Sherwood," she shrieked. "She's alone."

"Aye." He released her elbow, knowing she shan't run from him now. "I've beseeched her to take shelter in her root cellar if anything becomes amiss, but you know as well as I, how she's dominated by her routine. She's refused to leave her house."

"Oh, nay." She strode to his horse. "We must away. But what are we to do?" Her eyes searched his.

He wished he possessed the answers she sought. "I know not, besides pray for God's guidance."

She nodded, then allowed him to help her onto his horse "Look." He followed the direction of her finger. "They've begun setting fires."

His breath caught at the sight of the billowing smoke. "They've set Dr. Blackstone's home afire." His eyes sat transfixed on the blaze. *God, help us all.*

"I cannot see Dr. Blackstone." She squinted into the distance. "Surely, they shan't burn people in their beds?"

His heart hammered in his chest. "I pray not." But being turned out into the cold may not allow them to fare any better.

"Goodness me," she whispered under her breath, her eyes fixed on the burning house. "Cole." She pointed once more. "There's Edgar. He's come out of his house."

Cole mounted his horse. "He's alive. Now we must make certain Mrs. Sherwood is, as well."

"Wait." She grabbed his arm. He looked toward Dr. Blackstone again. The man's fists fought the air, and his angry wails carried across the land.

"Stop, Doctor!" he shouted. Either the doctor heard not or ignored his warning, because he ran at an American rearguard. His fists however never made contact with the soldier, as a blast sounded and sent up a cloud of smoke from the rearguard's musket. Dr. Blackstone's body slumped to the ground.

"Nay," she screamed. He held her. She shook under his embrace. "They killed him," she sobbed.

He squeezed her as if he could impart strength into her. "We cannot remain here."

"Nay." She trembled. "They've seen us. They shall come this way."

His eyes darted across the land. Uniforms marched through the snow.

"Hold on. We shan't risk our lives by staying here. This is war, and a bloody cruel one at that." He called to his horse and the wind howled past their ears, taking with it the sound of her crying. She may have detested Dr. Blackstone, but her tears proved this hadn't been the level of revenge she had wished. She wasn't as evil as she thought herself. Perhaps now she'd realize that fact. If not, he sat determined to make her accept that truth.

But, that must wait. Her cries faded under the sound of screams. Militiamen and Canadian Volunteers were everywhere, warning people and pointing out the approaching smoke.

"We're almost there." He guided his horse up the lane to Mrs. Sherwood's house. As they dismounted he thanked God it still stood.

"Mrs. Sherwood," she yelled as she threw open the front door.

"In the parlor, dear," Mrs. Sherwood sang, as if 'twere a carefree Friday morning and they had come for tea.

"Is all well?" She ran into the room and he trailed directly behind her.

"Aye. Some men came to scare me into leaving my home, but I sent them away." The widow took a bite of her biscuit. "The nerve, telling an old woman to leave her house. Do they not know how the cold would affect my health? Foolishness. Utter foolishness."

Her eyes shot to his. Indiscreetly, he waved her over to the opposite side of the room beside a window for a tête-à-tête. "I shall return in a moment," she told Mrs. Sherwood, then joined him in the corridor.

"We cannot remain here any longer," he whispered.

"I know." The anxious look on her face matched the roiling of his gut. "I shall do everything within my power to convince her to withdraw to her root cellar."

He shook his head. "'Tis not enough."

Her eyebrows plunged toward one another. "True, the root cellar is not a home, we shan't be able to manage over the winter."

"Even if we could, I cannot hide in her root cellar. The British shall take their land back, and if I'm found, they shall kill me."

"You're not to blame for this."

"But I'm American, they shan't ask questions before they react."

"We shan't abandon you." She stood firm and his heart squeezed. She did indeed care for him.

"Nor can I abandon you. Rebuilding this house would be too strenuous for Mrs. Sherwood, and you cannot do it alone."

"What are we to do then?"

He swallowed the lump in his throat. "Return to the United States."

Jamilyn's head involuntarily twitched to the left and right. Nay, she most definitely could not return. She had never planned on setting foot on American soil ever again.

"I'm sorry, but I promised your father I'd protect you, and keeping you with me is the only way I know of to do that."

"But," she stammered. How could he even suggest she return? "There must be somewhere else."

"I never wished this outcome either." His eyes softened. "But I cannot think of another plan to ensure our safety."

She trembled. "I cannot believe any of this is happening. 'Tis too much. And all too sudden."

"You need not return home." He held her stare. "Just cross the Niagara River into the United States."

She took a deep breath. "Fine. I suppose I'm not needed as a cook at the fort any longer." The pressure started to loosen around her chest. "And once we cross the river, we can send Mrs. Sherwood by coach to the Mohawk Valley to be with her daughter and son where she shall be safe. Neither of us need return home to New Callander."

His lip twitched up. "Correct."

She smiled back. "'Tis a fine plan, but it rests on us convincing Mrs. Sherwood."

"Not an easy task."

"Nay, I dare say it shan't be. But what other choice have we?"

"None." He stole her hand and squeezed it. "Nor do we have the luxury of time. The Rearguard may be here soon." She followed his gaze out the window. Thankfully all they saw—for now—were snowflakes.

"Cole." She pulled her hand away from his and crossed her arms as if to fend off the cold. "How shall people survive out of doors in this storm?"

"I pray they have family or friends out of town to whom they can travel."

"In this snow?" She grimaced, and he returned her look.

"Then, root cellars, or the ability to construct lean-tos from wood not touched by fire. Most shall not know to seek refuge in the stonehouse at Fort George. Being composed of rock, that building shan't burn."

"We must tell them, and help as many people as possible."

"I agree, but we must move Mrs. Sherwood from here first."

"Aye. But, what to do or say to convince her to follow us, I haven't a clue. I know not whether she holds dearly to her routine, or, if after what she's experienced, she simply cannot handle any more change."

"I cannot blame her. This war has seen her family torn apart. First, her son was taken as a prisoner of war, then her husband died. Next, her daughter entered enemy territory to find her brother, Mrs. Sherwood's son. And now, her house may be burned to the ground, and she must abandon it, along with all her worldly possessions."

She took another deep breath. "God, please help us. We sincerely need it," her eyes looked up as she prayed. "Let us not delay a moment longer." He dipped his chin. "Mrs. Sherwood," she oozed sweetness, as she calmly approached the widow. "Have you finished your tea?"

"Aye, 'twas lovely." The widow smiled. "Tastes much better now that I'm well and can enjoy it in my favorite room."

She nodded and forced her lips upward. "I understand you delight in your needlepoint work now, but that must wait until tomorrow."

"Tomorrow? Oh, goodness, nay. I must put in a good day's work every day if I'm to finish this embroidery for my daughter by Christmas."

She looked to him for help. "Mrs. Sherwood," he spoke softly. "Would it please you to spend this Christmas with your daughter and son?"

"I would love nothing more, but 'tis impossible. Do you not forget they're in the Mohawk Valley of the United States, a country we're at war with?"

"Do you not forget, Jamilyn and I are Americans, we can take you there to enjoy Christmas with both your son and daughter."

"'Tis very kind of you to offer." She graced him with a smile. "But 'tis such a long way."

"Pish," she cut in. "You'd arrive in a day or two."

"Bless you, but this old woman was born and raised in this very house and I shan't leave my home."

"I understand your attachment to it," she tried to keep her voice calm, but even she heard her desperate lilt. "You heard what the soldiers said, they're to come and burn it down."

"You believe them?" Violet clucked her tongue. "I shall make certain 'tis not you who answers the door to a travelling salesman or you shall lose all your money."

He rubbed his forehead. "Mrs. Sherwood, those American soldiers, came with the express purpose of trying to save your life from fire."

"Pray tell why would our enemy care to save our lives?" she snickered.

"They're God-fearing men. They wish not to have the deaths of so many innocent people on their hands."

"If you believe that, I'm afraid you've been fooled. Those men merely wish me out of my house to pillage it."

"Mrs. Sherwood," he spoke under his breath to contain his irritation. "If those men desired your belongings they may have easily barged in and taken them. They're armed and know how

to fight. You'd never have been able
to stop them."

The woman's hand flew to her
chest. "I say, there is no need to
insult me."

He let out a slow breath. "I
apologize. That wasn't my intention. I
mean for you to understand, that
unfortunately, I know soldiers on both
sides of this war who take liberties
where they ought not."

"Do you remember Fiona
Robertson?" she asked, tearing
Violet's hurt expression away from
him.

"Aye." She nodded. "Her late aunt
was a good friend of mine."

"The American soldiers would have
pillaged her homestead this past
summer if it weren't for her friend,
Lachlan McAllister, an American
officer, who stopped them."

"But even he couldn't stop them
from seizing her house, wrecking her
fencing for fire wood, and butchering
her livestock for food," he added.

"Humph," Mrs. Sherwood snorted.
"That lass did endure a terrible
ordeal."

Her heart hurt for Fiona—and for what she had done to her. Somehow and someday, she'd make amends. "Aye." She knelt in front of Violet's chair and took her hand. "Please know our reason for telling you this is that we don't wish you to endure any more suffering."

Tears welled in Mrs. Sherwood's eyes. She patted her hand. They need not speak, everyone knew Mrs. Sherwood had undergone too much grief in such a short period.

"Mrs. Sherwood," she cooed, knowing they had finally penetrated her barrier. "We must leave now."

"Nay." Mrs. Sherwood threw her hand in the air and sent her aback. "I shan't leave my home."

On the brink of tears she glanced at him. But her frustration was useless. She knew what must be done. Their attempt to convince Violet had failed. Forget niceties or explanations. This lady must come with them for her own good whether she agreed or not.

"Mrs. Sherwood, we cannot remain here," she announced. "I shall pack your things. Either you help or I shall choose among your items. Your daughter entrusted me to care for you and I shall not betray her trust in me." She strode from the room without responding to Violet's vehement protestations.

"Tallyho," he whispered as he followed her.

She blushed. "We needed a different approach, talking apparently failed miserably."

"Leave it to you." He winked. "Now, what do you wish me to pack." They rushed upstairs and threw Mrs. Sherwood's belongings in a sack.

"She keeps her valuables in here." She pulled out a satchel and stuffed that in the sack as well, then she rushed to her own bedroom and packed her belongings. "Do you need help packing?" she asked.

"I need only the clothes on my back, which is just as well, since you've provided more than enough for me to carry," he teased as he held up the sacks.

She grinned. Grateful for his presence in yet another crisis. "Did you hear that?" Her face fell.

"Aye." He rushed to the window. "The rearguards have come."

amilyn's heart stopped at Cole's declaration that the rearguards had come to Mrs. Sherwood's house. "We must away, now."

"Aye." He hurried from the room and down the stairs straight into the front entrance vestibule where he dropped the two sacks. "Jamilyn, please bundle yourself as warm as possible and then we shall see to Mrs. Sherwood."

She didn't hesitate. She had already experienced the frigid weather, and knowing not how long they'd be out of doors again in this storm, she grabbed everything she could to insulate herself.

"Mrs. Sherwood," he called, after he had applied layers of clothes to himself. "Please join us in the front entrance vestibule?"

"Certainly," the widow responded.

"Jamilyn, these sacks are heavy, but are you able to carry them?"

She yanked them off the floor. "They're manageable," she grunted.

He grinned. "I hope you do indeed know I hold you in the highest esteem."

"You beckoned," Mrs. Sherwood rounded the corner, then stopped immediately once she saw them in their outer garments. "Are you to brave this weather?" She eyed the sacks.

"Aye." He stepped in behind her to dissuade her from fleeing. "And you shall come, as well."

"What?" Violet spun on her heal and bumped into the wall he had fashioned himself into. "What is the meaning of this?" Terror lit her face. "Are you taking me captive?"

"Mrs. Sherwood, American soldiers have come. You must put on your coat." She draped the garment over the widow's shoulders.

"But—" Mrs. Sherwood attempted to shrug it off.

She held it firmly in place. "I promise, this is for your own good."

"I fail to see how that is possible. I'm not a child. You cannot force me to abide by your decisions against my wishes." She pointed her finger at each of them in turn. "You ought to be in fear of imprisonment for such an assault against me," she hissed at him. "And to think, I invited you into my home." She stomped her foot and turned to Jamilyn. "And you, you ought to fear my daughter's rebuke. I believe you shall lose the only friend you possess."

That comment speared her heart. Penny was indeed her sole friend.

"I'm sorry." He fastened the top button of Mrs. Sherwood's coat. "But we must save talk of this until later. You must dress for the icy weather we're to face."

"Well, I never," Violet huffed, as he pulled her hood on.

"'Tis for your own good, Mrs. Sherwood," she repeated, her nerves wrought for the distressed woman.

"Pray tell, what is that smell?" Mrs. Sherwood's nose twitched. "Did one of you forget to tend the fire in the kitchen? I smell smoke."

The alarm she felt raced across his face. "Nay," he took hold of Mrs. Sherwood's arm to stop her from running toward the blaze. "The rearguards have set fire to your house."

"Such foolish nonsense," the widow scoffed. "I assure you 'tis a small difficulty with the chimney. This has happened before, and I dare say it shall happen again. Now, if you please unhand me, I shall mend the problem myself before the entire house burns down."

"I'm sorry." He pulled Mrs. Sherwood to the front door and swung it open. "'Tis not your chimney. See for yourself."

Mrs. Sherwood gasped as an American soldier trudged through the snow in front of her house carrying a torch. "Get out, unless you wish to burn," the rearguard shouted, then leaned his firebrand toward a pillar and set it aflame.

Violet swayed, but he caught her. No one deserved such treatment, especially Mrs. Sherwood. She'd had so much taken from her already. Her heart beat wildly with anger.

"The sacks, Jamilyn" he called over his shoulder as he grabbed Mrs. Sherwood up into his arms. She didn't hesitate and stepped out of the warmth of the widow's beloved home into the freezing cold.

"Nay," Mrs. Sherwood cried as she beat her fists into his chest. But he held her, unyielding. She could only pray that years of not performing manual labor proved her hits softer then they appeared. If not, hopefully his greatcoat had been fashioned from a very heavy wool that cushioned the woman's blows.

"My home," Violet wailed. "What am I to do now?" Tears streamed down the widow's cheeks, and she clenched the sacks tighter, her heart ached for her. "Where are we to go?"

"To the river," he spoke stoically. "We shall board a boat waiting to ferry Americans across."

"But I'm not American," Mrs. Sherwood sobbed.

"You shall be an exception." He glanced over his shoulder at her. "Are you able to carry the sacks that far?"

"Aye." She stiffened her arms. She'd bear the weight of the burden or die in her attempt.

"Oh, dear," Mrs. Sherwood exclaimed. "Cole, lay me upon my feet this instant. You must help her. I shall walk."

He eyed the widow and the serious look on her face must have convinced him for he gently placed her feet on the snow covered ground. "Thank you for hauling them thus far." He took the sacks as if they weighed little more than cups of tea.

Her arms whimpered with pleasure before she caught hold of Mrs. Sherwood to aid her navigation through the deep snow.

"Well I never. All these homes destroyed." Mrs. Sherwood's head flew from right to left. "The whole town must be aflame."

"Aye." Her nose wrinkled at the smell of billowing smoke.

"Is there naught we can do to help?" The widow's sorrow shone from her eyes.

"If you wish, you may provide them your horses to transport them to safety on farms farther away." She patted her back, urging her forward as she consoled her.

"Aye, please do." Mrs. Sherwood stopped. "I cannot bear to leave whilst people suffer."

"We best continue moving." He shifted the sacks in his hands for a better grip. "This entire area shall smolder come noon."

She pulled away from Mrs. Sherwood's hold. "Cole, take the sacks

and Mrs. Sherwood to the boat, I shall
meet you there once I offer what help
I can."

"Nay," he commanded.

But she had already backed away.
"Cole, the rearguards shall set fire
to the stable any moment. I must free
the horses."

"I've already released them from
their stalls."

"But they still may become
trapped in the stable," she insisted.
"I promise, I shall meet you at the
river in a few minutes. I shan't be
far behind you."

"Nay," he increased his emphatic
declaration, but she ran in the
opposite direction. She must help
those horses, and if possible, the
people of Newark.

Cole watched as Jamilyn ran from
them. He dropped the sacks to catch
her. "Let her be," Mrs. Sherwood
reached out for him, but her legs
caught in the snow and she tumbled
face first into the cold surface.

"Mrs. Sherwood!" He pulled her
from the white heap.

"I'm fine." The woman shivered. Jamilyn was now several yards away. He sighed. He'd be unable to catch her now. *God be with her*. He turned his attention back to Mrs. Sherwood. He must tend to her. She'd never survive the journey to the river without him. *God, please bring Jamilyn back safely.* He grabbed the sacks. *But if You cannot, then please help me guide Mrs. Sherwood to a boat so I may find Jamilyn myself.*

"Stay behind me, Mrs. Sherwood." He stomped down the snow in front of her. "I shall forge a path for you to follow."

She agreed, and they plodded down to the Niagara River. The scent of burning wood assaulted his nose. 'Twas as if an entire forest had been set aflame.

He glanced over his shoulder at Mrs. Sherwood. The day shone as bleak as her thoughts must be. If only they had been like the sun, and had managed to stay away, then they too should have avoided witnessing all this destruction.

God, please show mercy to all these destitute people, he prayed as they approached the river and he searched for a boat.

"Sam," he called. "Are you to travel across the river?"

"Aye." The guard handed his son to his wife, who stood in a boat. The woman caught hold of their son and steadied him until he found his sea legs.

"Is there room on your boat for my good friend, Mrs. Sherwood?" He smiled in her direction. "She must travel to America?"

"Aye, we've room enough for several others. Are you to come?"

"I cannot." He handed him the sacks after Sam had gone aboard. "I must find Jamilyn first."

"She's not here?" Sam's concern for the fort's cook touched him.

"She was determined to offer aid first."

"For her own safety, you had best instruct her to forgo such heroism. The Militiamen and Canadian Volunteers have already traveled across the river. It shan't be long before the

Rearguard depart, as well. Then there shall be no one left to defend Americans when the British come. And look upon all the fire and smoke behind you, the British would be daft to miss such a spectacle. They shall approach before long."

He knew the man spoke the truth and grimaced at the destruction. "Mrs. Sherwood, you shall be safe with Sam and his family." He handed her over to the guard. "Sam, please send Mrs. Sherwood to the Hilltop Inn." Sam nodded and he met Mrs. Sherwood's eyes. "We shall meet you there."

"Please, hurry." Mrs. Sherwood sat in the boat. "I'm to blame if Jamilyn is hurt."

"Nay." His fists clenched. "'Tis I, and only I, who shall assume responsibility for her."

"I ought not to have mentioned the horses," Mrs. Sherwood mumbled.

"She shall be fine. I shall deliver her to safety." He squared his shoulders. "Fret not. You mustn't forget that to which you constantly remind me, *give your worries to the Lord, He shall take care of you.*"

"Aye." Mrs. Sherwood nodded with a smile. "I shall pray until we meet again."

He dipped his chin. They needed those prayers more than ever, as he ran toward the blazing inferno.

Jamilyn rushed to the stable. The same Rearguard who had set Mrs. Sherwood's house on fire marched toward it, his torch held high in his right hand. "Stop," she yelled. The man did not so much as flinch. "You shan't set that stable on fire." She caught up to him.

The man growled, "Get away with you." Then, as he turned to see who had yelled at him, he nearly knocked her down with his torch wielding arm.

"I shall, after I free those horses." She ran ahead.

"I cannot allow that." The man bolted past her. "We're to burn everything to deny the British military shelter and resources. Those horses are too great an asset."

She gasped at the monster beside her. "Over my dead body." She quickened her pace.

"That is within my power to arrange if you insist on this interference." The Rearguard swung his firebrand toward her.

She jumped out of its path. Determination settled into her bones, she would set those horses free. She reached for the latch to open the stable door. "Unhand me," she screamed as the man grabbed her arm and yanked her away.

"I shall. But after I set the stable afire," the man sneered.

His grip caused her flesh to ache as she struggled to free herself. "Stop," she screamed. He failed to heed her, and appeared as if he hadn't even heard her. "You ought not murder them," she seethed. He reached out his torch to ignite the wooden stable wall.

"What is the meaning of this?"

Her head swung toward the male voice. "Cole!" She squirmed in the Rearguard's hold. "Help, he's about to set fire to the stable and kill the horses."

"No doubt he is, cook." He sauntered over to them. Her jaw fell lax. Why was he not attempting to stop this lunatic? "We are in a war against the British." He chucked her chin with a wink.

"You think she'd understand," the guard sneered. "She *is* an American after all."

"Aye." He grabbed her by the waist and pulled her away from the rearguard. "I shall see to her." He gazed upon her with a fierce look.

"Good." The rearguard touched his torch to the stable and waited for the wood to ignite. "We cannot allow Americans to position the needs of animals ahead of their own people."

She opened her mouth to speak, but he slammed his hand over top. "Fine work on this property, but I shall finish that to which you've begun." She thrashed against his tyranny. "The rearguard have proceeded to the river and the boats are being loaded rather quickly."

The rearguard's face flushed with fear. "I shan't be caught on this side of the river."

"Nay, that would result in certain death."

"Yours, as well," her words were unintelligible as they jumbled themselves into his hand.

"You'd best accompany me," the rearguard urged, then glanced at her. "Her, as well."

"We shall be directly upon your heals," he assured him. "Please, do save us two spots upon your boat."

"As you wish. But I shan't be able to save them long." He walked backwards. "I don't fancy being shot dead in the water."

"Nay," he dipped his chin, before the rearguard turned and trotted toward the river.

"Unhand me!" her words finally became intelligible once he had released her. "Was that necessary?" She glared at him.

"I believed so."

She huffed, then ran to the stable door. "The horses!" She undid the latch.

He rushed through the open door and soon horses galloped out.

She counted them as they passed. Only one remained. But why the delay? "Cole," she shouted into the smoke.

"Get out! The fire's reached the roof. The entire building shall collapse."
     No answer.

The stable roof creaked. "Cole!" Jamilyn yelled over the flames. The final horse bolted past her. She jumped to the side, barely avoiding being trampled. "Cole," she screamed.

He still didn't appear.

God, I need You. She covered her mouth with her handkerchief and rushed into the stable. "Cole? I cannot see you." The smoke hung thick and its pungency stung her eyes and caused them to water. She stretched out a hand and felt the first stall gate. Holding on, she walked sideways, farther into the stable.

"Cole!" her voice squawked, drowned by the fabric over her lips. Terror seized her. Perhaps a beam had fallen on him. She removed the handkerchief and shouted his name again.

A cough croaked through the smoke, then another, and another, each louder than their predecessor. "Jamilyn, get out," his hoarse voice scarcely resembled him.

"Not without you." She felt about for him. Wood scraped her fingers. "Ouch." She jerked her hand back, but continued. Hang any cuts, bruises, scrapes or slivers she may incur, pain wouldn't stop her. "Cole?" She fisted some woolen fabric.

"Aye." His hand slid up her arm. She clung to him and ambled toward the exit. Another loud creak sent her heart thundering against her chest. *Please, God, hold up the roof.*

"We're nearly there." She had never welcomed the smell of frosty air more, and quickened her pace. "Oh, nay," she mumbled when his body tugged at her. He pulled her back and slowed their progress. She thought he had been the one to lead, but in fact, it had been her who had dragged him. *Thank You for the strength, God.*

She held him tighter. He coughed several times as she pulled him toward the opening. "Make haste," she pleaded. His attempt wilted when something snagged his foot and he fell.

They hadn't come this far to die. "Move," she groaned, and grabbed him from behind. Twining her hands under his arms, she linked them across his chest, and pulled with all her might. *Please, God.* She dragged him over the threshold. Lugging him away from the flames she fell into the snow beside him. Her chest heaved as she panted, and they both watched as the roof caved in.

"You saved my life." He took her hand, his hazel eyes soft with appreciation.

Her lips rose slyly. "I suppose 'tis only fair then, that we split a portion of the money my pa pays you."

"I never claimed your pa paid me."

Her head shot up. "Aye, you did. You stated rather clearly that he had commissioned you."

"He did," his words flowed slowly. "But I never specified that I had accepted payment."

"But, surely, you intend to." She stared at him. However, he never met her eyes.

He shrugged a shoulder. "Nay. I was glad for an excuse to leave home." Her lips parted, but her words choked in her throat. He had watched over her for months, with such intensity, for nothing. "But—" she bit her lip when he sat clutching his ribs with a groan "—pray tell, what befell you in there?" She sprang to her feet and offered him her hand.

He abided, and with some effort, rose to his feet. "The last horse. 'Twas scared, and reared up and kicked me in the chest." His weight pulled her to him. She gasped when their bodies collided. She had never been this close to him—or any man, besides her pa, and this felt much different. Her eyes held his, and everything around them faded into the snow.

"I didn't intend to hurt you, please tell me I didn't?" his words swirled toward her like flakes from a snow drift scattered wildly by the wind.

She shook her head, both to answer his question and to set her mind right. "Ahem," she coughed, then stepped backwards awkwardly. How long had they been that close? She ought to have pulled away sooner. Nay, she ought to have pulled away immediately. She chastised herself more as she looked toward the smoldering stable. The temperature had fallen well below zero, but she fanned herself.

"We ought to go." He stepped in behind her and rested his hands on her shoulders.

He must think her flustered from the wreckage. She forced herself to smile and turned to face him. "Aye, indeed. We must join Mrs. Sherwood."

"I fear we shan't find her until we land on American soil. I've sent her thus with Sam and his family, and given him instructions to send her to the closest inn."

She nodded as she hugged herself. "Then we must leave before the British arrive."

"Aye, we neither of us need to once more be in the throes of death."

"Are you able to walk?"

"Aye." He grimaced as they strode forth.

She forced down her thoughts and emotions as she held him. "Are you in much pain?" She avoided touching the side that bothered him most.

"Only when I breath." He gave her a lopsided grin. Perhaps she ought to have laughed, but she had busied herself in an attempt to convince herself he hadn't affected her.

"Wait." She bounded away from him and bent down to grab a long stick. "Here."

"Thank you." He leaned his weight on the cane. "That does indeed help."

"Oh, my." Her hand flew to her mouth as they neared the main section of town—if it could still be thus named. "I cannot believe my eyes," she muttered. "Everything's been destroyed."

"Not everything." He pointed to some people constructing a lean-to out of timber that hadn't been completely burned. "The human spirit cannot be destroyed that quickly or easily."

She looked with awe at him. How had he seen something positive amid all this devastation? All she saw were scanty shacks swaying against still-standing chimneys. *God, please keep these people safe and warm until the British soldiers come to help.* "Please help me spread word," she called to a middle-aged man about to pass them. "People may find shelter at Fort George, the stonehouse there remains standing."

"Thank you," the man dipped his chin and trotted away.

"We must walk by that family." She motioned in the direction of a couple huddled together to fend off the cold from their baby. "Are you acquainted with Mrs. Sherwood?"

The mother nodded. "How has she fared?"

"Fine. She's to leave town, as are we," she spoke fast, knowing they must cross the river soon before the British came upon them, which could be any time. They had already overshot their allotted time. And she wouldn't be the cause of Cole's death. "On Mrs. Sherwood's property, you may find her team of horses roaming about. Please, take one and ride to a nearby farmhouse for shelter."

"We couldn't possibly," the man began to protest.

"Nonsense, she most ardently wishes to help anyone in need."

"But how shall we ever repay her?" the woman asked with tears in her eyes.

"Merely help others along the way. Tell whomever needs a horse where to retrieve one or to seek shelter at Fort George." She slowed her steps. "Oh, and there's a root cellar on Mrs. Sherwood's property, behind whatever remains of her house, if anyone wishes shelter there."

"God bless you," the woman hugged her baby tighter.

"Aye, and God be with you in your travels," her husband croaked with gratitude. She merely nodded to them both and walked on. She hadn't heard such blessings directed at her before from strangers.

"We're nearly there." He broke her reverie and she hastened her steps.

"Wonderful, for I believe you need to sit." She took his arm. "Are you in more pain?"

"I'd rather not speak of it, so I may pretend otherwise," he hissed through gritted teeth.

"I understand." She pointed to a boat crossing the river. "That nasty rearguard's in a boat by himself."

"I shan't have ever imagined he'd have waited for us. But to aid no one else," he pursed his lips. "No matter, God's provided for us. There's a canoe."

"Thank You, God." She followed him down a path to the water's edge.

"I do pray God provides for these poor people, as well." She looked back at the devastation.

"He shall." He helped her into the vessel.

She sighed. "I do so hope you're correct." The boat rocked and her stomach flipped. "I shan't appreciate plunging into the coldness of that water."

"Nor I." He boarded the boat, wincing in pain.

"Sit." She picked up an oar. "I shall paddle."

"These waters are rough." He picked up the other oar. "But I dare say I know better than to cross you."

"Finally." She grinned.

He chuckled. "However, you shall require help."

"I shan't allow you to further injure yourself."

"Thank you. But I see a rearguard walking along the shore, surely you shan't object to his help?"

"Certainly not."

He shouted to the rearguard. When the man neared them, he said, "Perhaps we may benefit one another. I'm injured and wish your help paddling across the river."

"Boats are becoming scarce. Thank you. I'd rather not risk swimming across the river." He shivered, then found his seat. Once they had pushed away from the shore, he rowed with the might of five men. She pumped her arms to the best of her ability and thankfully her effort didn't cause them to spin in circles.

"Land ho," he cried out an encouraging cheer as their canoe neared the shore.

"Thank You, God." She breathed in the smoky air, as the rearguard jumped out to pull them in. "I still cannot believe all that happened this morning." She remained motionless, even after the rearguard bid them farewell and headed to Fort Niagara. Her eyes remained on the ruins across the water.

"I wish the destruction had never occurred." He shook his head at the smoldering horror they had left behind. "For the rest of my days, I shall pray for those people."

"I, as well." She finally tore her eyes away to glance at him. *Thank You, Lord, for seeing him out alive.* Then she squealed, "Mrs. Sherwood! She's alone. We must away."

"Aye. She's suffered too much. And she certainly shall be happy to lay eyes on your familiar face."

"Yours, as well, I dare say." She stood and attempted to maintain her balance as she stepped out of the canoe.

He grabbed her elbow to prevent her from falling into the water. "Do be careful."

"Thank you," she uttered with a sorrowful grimace once he clenched his jaw to suppress pain. "I'm sorry."

"'Tis not your fault."

She looked at him doubtfully. No part of her believed him. She swung on her heal, embarrassed she had needed the help of an injured man. But, her foot slipped and she fell faster than an osprey hawk diving into the water to catch a fish.

He knelt beside her before she even knew what had happened. "Are you hurt?"

"My ankle." She grabbed it whilst she attempted to hold back tears.

"Are you able to stand?" He held out his hand to help her up.

"I believe so." She cringed. "But, perhaps in a moment." She bit down hard on her lip and forced her body up.

"Fine pair we make." He clung to her as much as she clung to him.

She laughed. "Perhaps Mrs. Sherwood shall be able to help us."

"Aye, she's stronger than she thinks." He grinned. "But, alas, we must reach her first." He looked about. "There's a wagon for hire. That ought to deliver us to the inn."

"If we're able to move thus far." She smiled up into his hazel eyes.

"Oh, I do believe you're more than capable. Anyone who'd attempt to fight off a cougar shan't easily be kept from anything she sets her mind to."

"Thank you. I would curtsey. However, I best save my strength, or at least not injure myself further. But I ought to say the same for you. We both of us shan't allow a few broken bones or sprains to stop us, shall we?"

"Nay. Especially when I know the inn to be in possession of refreshments."

"Aye." She closed her eyes to dream about a feast. "I've not consumed anything since drinking Doctor Blackstone's medicine last night."

"Then my dear lady, let us not delay." His jaw tightened under a smile as they began to walk. She marveled at his ability to laugh in the face of pain. Perhaps to remain sane, the skill had been established after his brother's death—a death she truly wished to learn of in more detail, for her desire to help him had grown immensely strong.

"Jamilyn! Cole," Mrs. Sherwood hustled through the inn's crowded public room, past the multitude of long tables with benches positioned around the outskirts. "I've been beside myself with worry." She hugged them together. "Cole?" She jumped back when he moaned. "You're injured." The din from the other patrons nearly drowned her shouting voice.

"A horse, he saved, kicked him in the chest," she informed her.

Horrified, Mrs. Sherwood rubbed his shoulder. "That ungrateful beast."

"Nay, 'twas merely afraid." He shook off her sympathy.

But she wouldn't allow him to elude the appreciation he deserved. "That horse fared well thanks to you risking your life running into that burning stable."

"My stable?" Violet's hand flew to her chest.

"Aye," he nodded. "I'm sorry we failed to save it."

"But, all your animals fled alive, thanks to Cole," she interposed.

"Thanks to you," he retorted with a look to Mrs. Sherwood. "When I came upon her, I found her standing her ground fighting a rearguard to save the animals' lives."

Mrs. Sherwood leaned forward and hugged them once more, but stopped when his face twitched in anticipation of pain. "God bless you both."

She froze. Two times in one day. Besides her pa, she had never felt blessed by God. Suppose He listened to these people.

"Come, sit, you must be in need of some nourishment." Through the dimly lit room, Mrs. Sherwood motioned them to the nearest table. "Jamilyn, you're limping." The widow grabbed her arm and helped her slide into the bench.

"I shall be fine, I assure you." She sat. "I merely slipped on ice and twisted my ankle."

Violet eyed her leg. "Are you certain you didn't break your bone?"

"Aye." She stretched her leg. "See, I'm able to move—" she gritted her teeth as she substantiated her claim "—however, I prefer not to. I believe it hurts worse than a kick from a horse to the chest." She dared a smile at him.

"And you would know this how?" He smirked.

She shrugged a shoulder. "Extraordinary perception."

"Or misperception?"

"Now, now, you two." Mrs. Sherwood clucked her tongue, then called the hostess. "Eat and drink. We shall each benefit from a good night sleep before we set off on our journey to New Callander tomorrow."

"New Callander," she shrieked. Several patrons turned, including Mrs. Sherwood and Cole.

"Aye." Mrs. Sherwood said, her face contorted into astonishment, as if she wore a snake on her head. "I confess, this morning I had been in a fair bit of shock, but I do clearly remember you promised to deliver me to my daughter and son."

"Aye. We promised to deliver you to them, but we never promised to join you on the journey." She looked to him for support. Surely, given how insistent he had been about not setting foot in the Mohawk Valley, he'd help set Mrs. Sherwood straight. But he hesitated. He merely opened his mouth, then closed it again.

She pursed her lips, then turned back to Mrs. Sherwood. "I'm sorry if you misunderstood, but the impossibility of such a journey—why 'tis—well, 'tis simply impossible."

"How can that be so?" Mrs. Sherwood eyed her. "I should think you'd be only too happy to see your father again. I know he'd love nothing more than to hold you in his arms. And with Christmas a mere fortnight away, I cannot believe you don't wish to be home."

She swallowed the lump in her throat and blinked back tears. Aye, she ardently desired to see her pa. She wished more than anything in the world to return home. But she couldn't. She couldn't face the people of New Callander. They did not wish her there. She no longer belonged there.

She glanced back at him. Unable to speak, she needed him to explain their situation to Mrs. Sherwood. If anyone could help Violet to understand, he could. He did indeed enjoy playing with words to get his way. And she nearly smiled at the thought of their first meeting near Fort George—how he had tried, so many

times, to turn the conversation away
from what she had demanded to know.

When he opened his mouth to
speak, she sat forward with eagerness.
Finally, he'd put an end to this
nonsense. "We must return home."

ad that horse kicked Cole in the chest or his head? "Cole?" Jamilyn's eyebrows pinched together as she pierced his name. "You must be in need of sleep. You cannot mean—"

"I understand your reluctance to return home, and how much it pains you, but I cannot conceive of another alternative." His expression softened and the compassion in his eyes seared her.

"Plenty of choices may present themselves," she sputtered.

His head tilted in rebuttal. "I fail to see any." He took her hand. "My chest pains me to breath, let alone walk. And I shan't even dare attempt to bend over. Then there's your ankle. 'Tis impossible for you to walk without pain. Hence, even if 'twere possible to travel in this horrid weather, how would we survive? We're both unfit to find work."

"But," she stammered.

"We need not stay in New Callander forever. Just until we heal."

She pulled her hand away in horror. "That could amass weeks."

"Aye," he resigned his voice with the sag of his shoulders, then reached out to hold her hand once more. "I believe we're strong enough to prevail. Together." He squeezed her fingers. She couldn't look away from his imploring eyes.

"I know not why you're both this hesitant to return to your families, but you shall have me there, as well. And after all you've done for me, I shall try, for the rest of my life, to repay you." Mrs. Sherwood placed her hand over theirs and looked between them with such love and concern.

"I may hold you both to your promises." She put her other hand on top of the pile.

"Please do." Mrs. Sherwood added her left hand.

"I expect nothing less." He topped the hand tower.

She breathed deep. She now had two friends. But would that be enough to face the town?

*   *   *

"Let's stop here," Jamilyn talked over the horses' pounding hooves.

"But if we press on we shall arrive in New Callander to-night," Cole answered.

"I see no need to rush home," she purposely omitted how often she had seen him grit his teeth in agony throughout their wagon ride.

"I'm certainly in need of a nap." Mrs. Sherwood hid a yawn behind the back of her hand.

"That settles the matter then," she piped up. "Two out of three. You're outvoted."

He dipped his chin, then informed the driver of their request. Mrs. Sherwood closed her eyes, and he whispered to Jamilyn, "I'm glad we shall stop for the night. I too am less than eager to return home."

She smiled. To have someone secretly share her qualms soothed her. However, unlike her, he had done nothing wrong to fear the repercussions from the townspeople. Although, come to think of it, he hadn't told her *exactly* what had transpired with his brother. He was definitely hiding something.

"Cole, shall we warm ourselves with a hot cup of tea in the public room whilst Mrs. Sherwood naps?" Her muscles grew rigid. Oh, nay. He must think her interested in him and desirous of spending time alone with him. Sweat beaded on her forehead, even though the cold weather lashed at their wagon. Her plan to draw the truth out of him had been sorely misdirected.

"Only, if in addition to tea, I may partake in a meal, as well. I'm famished." He rubbed his belly. "And before you answer, please consider that food shall aid me in recovering faster."

"Certainly," she croaked with relief. "Whilst travelling, I suppose conventions need not be as stringent." He raised an eyebrow. Oh, dear. She had never flirted in her entire life, and now her every utterance sounded as such. "Those conventions pertaining to eating," she sputtered. Her cheeks flamed red. Such thoroughly, incomprehensible foolishness. Most unlike her.

But one look at him and she understood why she had become distraught—he had come to mean much more to her than simply someone she had known from the Mohawk Valley.

Not that she'd ever act on her feelings. She wasn't worthy of a man of his ilk. Her mother had turned to a life of sin, and she herself had chosen to do evil. She had hurt people—knowingly. But with God's help she'd help him. He didn't deserve a life in exile as she did.

Now, all she needed to do was induce him to confide in her the exact details surrounding his brother's death. She tapped her fingers on her skirt. She must know the particulars in order to help him. *Please, God, help me unravel this mystery for his sake.*

*   *   *

Cole looked about the inn's public room. Much nicer than the last one. The wooden tables wore linen tablecloths and were surrounded by chairs, even the floor didn't appear worn. A fire roared from a large hearth centered on the back wall of the room. The heat was immensely welcoming. Even the candles about the room added a touch of warmth that he stood grateful for. The seemliest quality though, was the general goodwill that permeated the room.

His stomach rumbled. This many cheerful people boded well for the food to fare better, as well. He grimaced at the remembrance of the cold, dry, lumpy porridge he had been forced to consume this morning before they had set off.

Inwardly he groaned, whether due to the thought of consuming more unpalatable food, or the fact that, despite his reluctance to be anywhere near the Mohawk Valley, he was indeed travelling in that very direction. But he shook off the thought. It mattered not. Their course had been set. And whatever the outcome, he'd be glad. He had finally convinced her to return home, where he'd aid her in making amends.

"M'lady." He pulled out a chair for her, but intense pains shot through his chest. He sagged down heavily into the chair. His fingers tightened into fists.

"Please don't trouble yourself on my account." She smiled and quickly

pulled out the chair beside him and
sat. "This journey has overtaxed you."
The distress in her stormy grey eyes
for his uneasiness further cemented
his resolve to help her. Although he
didn't need any further encouragement
on that subject. She was a good
person. She had proven it time and
again. What with her love for Mrs.
Sherwood, her drive to help the people
of Upper Canada and Mrs. Sherwood's
horses. She was a true Christian. Now,
if only he could impel her to see
herself as he did.

"How do you fare on this
journey?" He turned the tables.

She looked down at her foot. "My
ankle only hurts if I apply too much
weight. Hence, sitting in a wagon
allows me to forget my injury." She
smiled.

"I'm glad." He slowly raised
himself into more of an upright
position before he plunged into the
icy water. "But I meant to inquire
into how you're faring in terms of
returning home."

Her smile immediately dropped.
"I've resigned myself to my current

circumstance, but I've also devised a plan to maintain my sanity."

"Pray tell, I'd love to hear your plan. Perhaps I myself may benefit." He leaned forward, but the ache in his chest stopped him, and he sat back. Best to remain as still as possible for the time being.

"I plan to remain in my pa's home the entire time I'm in New Callander."

His eyebrows jerked up. "How shall you possibly manage such a feat?"

"Easy. I've nowhere to go and no one to see. And if I'm asked to leave the confines of my room, I shall simply tell the truth—I cannot due to my ankle. The more I rest, the quicker it shall heal. Thus, I do believe my plan ought to effect the same result for you, as well. Hence, you're welcome."

"Thank you. But after your ankle heals, what then?"

Her face conveyed her thought that he had just asked the silliest question in the history of mankind. "I shall leave New Callander and begin my life anew someplace else, where no one knows me or my family. And the days spent alone in my room shall offer plenty of time for me to sort through the particulars."

He nodded. "My plans include leaving the Mohawk Valley the minute my chest heals, as well. However, I know not what to do regarding Christmas? Certainly your father shan't allow you to remain locked in your room instead of attending church."

She chuckled. "As the pastor's daughter, I know a thing or two about hiding within the walls of a church." She peered down at her light blue skirt, then rubbed off an indiscriminate fleck. "I cannot tell you how many times I've attended church without anyone being the slightest bit aware of my presence."

"I shall feel the absence of your presence."

Her eyes darted up to meet his and a light beaconed from the grey within.

"That ought not to surprise you." He held her stare.

"Um," she hesitated. "I suppose not." She fiddled more with her skirt.

"Good, for if I must suffer through weeks of healing these ribs, I hoped to be accompanied with a friend by my side to help me pass the time."

"I shall write you letters," she said with an impish grin.

He narrowed his eyes, then shook his head. "You needn't bother. You shall find that even despite my broken bones I'm not a fair-weather friend. I shall knock on your door daily."

Her eyebrows slammed together. "Suppose I shan't answer?"

"You forget my father's profession? A spy. The apple doesn't fall far from the tree, you know."

"Aye. But just as I uncovered you in that bush, and nearly beat you, I cannot be held responsible if you surprise me and I once more hurt you."

"I shall consider myself warned." He smiled, then grew serious. "But I would much rather prefer you not hide yourself away. Truly, you need not."

She cocked an eyebrow. "I regret to inform you, you're sorely mistaken.

Perhaps you ought to ask Lachlan or Fiona to remind you."

"I have."

"What?" she barked, and fury clouded her eyes.

A slow smile slid across his lips. "Before I left New Callander to guard you, I happened to ask them if they'd ever consider forgiving you—that is, if I found you repentant." He paused to assess her reaction, and it did his heart good to see hope span her features.

But she crossed her arms, her face stricken serious, as she sat back, and asked, "And their response?"

"Fiona quoted Matthew, *For if ye forgive men their trespasses, your heavenly Father will also forgive you: But if ye forgive not men their trespasses, neither will your Father forgive your trespasses.*" She bit her lip, and her nostrils flared as she listened in silence. "And Lachlan was adamant you prove you're sorry."

"And how am I supposed to accomplish that?" she emphasized every word.

He laughed. "Apologize."

"Say a few words in remorse?" she shrilled with scorn.

"Aye, if your apology is sincere." He took a sip of the drink their hostess had brought them.

She exhaled the deep breath she had been holding. "I am sincere. But to face them? That I am thoroughly uncertain of," she mumbled so low he barely heard her above the din of the public room.

"I believe in you." He smiled and reached for her hand. And if you wish, I shall remain by your side as you offer your amends."

She pursed her lips together in a smile. "I appreciate that, but—" she looked down into her lap.

"But? There ought not be any rebuttal." He gently raised her chin.

"I'm sorry, I simply cannot," she spoke softly, not meeting his eyes.

"Why ever not?" He released his hold on her, as confusion contorted his mind. "Please do not say 'tis due to you still being in love with Lachlan and that you cannot bear to see him married to Fiona?" He shuffled about in his seat not caring as pains shot through him. Waiting for an answer he may never wish to hear hurt worse.

"Nay." She gasped. "'Tis not my reason at all." Her grey eyes met his and he couldn't bite back the irritation that crawled over his skin. Either he had just disturbed a bee hive or he had begun to care for her in a way that he most certainly ought not.

"Then please, explain."

"I cannot. The embarrassment would prove torturous."

"I fail to understand your distress. Are you embarrassed to admit you made a mistake or do you harbor another reason for this embarrassment?"

"I don't wish to discuss my reason." She nonchalantly picked up her drinking glass.

He coughed. If she were ever to apologize, he must persuade her to discuss this. "Jamilyn, I know you're sorry. Pray tell, how shall I convince you to apologize? I'd do anything."

Her mouth puckered. "Tell me your secret."

"What?" he spat, every muscle in his body solidified into ice. "I fail to understand the connection."

"Allow me to explain. I know you're eager to help me, but what you fail to realize is that I'm just as keen to help you, and I shan't allow you to help me if I'm not granted the courtesy to reciprocate."

"Nonsense." He shook his head.

"Be that as it may." She sat back, a look of smug satisfaction on her pretty face. "But I'm determined to help you, and I cannot offer my assistance unless you confide the entire story to me."

"'Tis extortion."

"Perhaps. But such are my terms." She leaned forward. "Hence, the question is, how much do you truly wish to save me?"

He shook his head. "I severely underestimated you." She laughed, and he could no longer begrudge her. "Fine." He narrowed his eyes. "But I have my own condition."

"Which is?" She crossed her arms and sat back.

He grinned. "Tomorrow is Sunday."

"Aye." She glared at him.

"I wish us to arrive in New Callander before church ends. Everyone shall be in attendance and you may then apologize all at once and be done with the matter."

She gasped. "You wish to torture me? Is this the thanks you bestow upon me for my attempt to help you?"

"It shan't be as bad as you think," he responded calmly. "And I do believe this agreement renders us fair."

"Fair?" She snorted with exasperation. "I must face the entire town."

He waved his hand in the air. "If you wish not to accept these terms—"

"Oh, I accept." She snickered, and stared at him hard. "I shan't allow you to abscond with ease."

He laughed. "I thought as much."

*   *   *

Jamilyn's stomach roiled the entire journey home—or, more accurately, to the lion's den. Her head hurt from crashing into every possible, disastrous outcome. She rubbed her clammy hands and glanced at Cole. His light brown hair shone in the sunlight, his hazel eyes reflected the wondrous sky, and his sturdy body emitted an air of strength. If he harbored even a shred of fear to return home he had buried his trepidation in the deepest depths of his being, for he showed absolutely no outward sign. But, perhaps he excelled at hiding his emotions.

He flashed his white teeth. Embarrassed he had caught her staring at him, she smiled, then quickly looked away. She'd uncover his true feelings soon enough. Immediately after she apologized to Lachlan and Fiona she'd demand he confide in her the reason he had left the Mohawk Valley. And God willing, she'd help him. She'd finally render her pa proud.

Her eyes misted as the town of New Callander appeared before them. The people here were definitely preparing to celebrate the birth of Jesus. The inn, decorated with its familiar evergreen boughs, stood in sharp contrast to the snow covered ground and rooftops. The general store displayed its goods to tempt the local women to begin their holiday baking. The post office's windowsills presented bouquets of pine branches. The schoolhouse offered a glimpse at the children's Christmas crafts. The tailor's shop hung a large Christmas quilt for all to admire. And the drug store's red bows with long ribbons swayed in the wind.

But her breath caught at her pa's church. The old building she had known had been burned to the ground, and this one had been erected after she had left for Upper Canada. The description her pa wrote in his letters failed to do it justice. The beauty of the white walls were emphasized in the front by two arched windows that flanked a matching wooden arched door. More arched windows graced the sides and the spire rose up to touch the sky and beacon parishioners with its cross.

"'Tis beautiful," she murmured as she wiped away tears. "My pa built that crèche," she informed her travel companions. "He labored for many months when I was a wee lass. I attempted to help—" she chuckled "—but I fear I was a hindrance, especially when I'd hurt myself." She bit back more tears as she remembered how patient and kind her pa had been. He had always kissed her injuries and encouraged her. "He's rather fond of quoting Philippians, *I can do all things through Christ which strengtheneth me.*" She swallowed the lump in her throat.

"I am indeed eager to meet with your father again. He's such a dear man." Mrs. Sherwood patted her hand. She returned her pleasant smile.

"Shan't be long now." He eyed her.

She shifted in her seat. She didn't wish to think about her encounter with Lachlan and Fiona. "Your children shall be ecstatic to see you, Mrs. Sherwood."

"Not nearly as excited as I am." Violet clapped her hands. "Oh, what a surprise this shall be!"

He grinned at her enthusiasm. "You shall be their most treasured Christmas present ever."

"I hear singing." She closed her eyes, and her heart filled with its message. "This may be the final song."

"Aye." Mrs. Sherwood surprised them both as she jumped down from the wagon akin to a woman half her age. "I cannot wait to behold my babies."

She smiled, but looked away when her thoughts turned inward. How different her life may have been if her mother had loved her with the same strength that Mrs. Sherwood loved her adopted children.

"Jamilyn," his voice woke her from her reverie. "'Tis time." He stood with his hand up, ready to help her down from the wagon. She hadn't even seen him lower himself to the ground.

Dismayed at what was to come, she nodded anyway. With God's help, she could do this. She squared her shoulders. Even if the worst happened and Lachlan and Fiona spat in her face, she'd know she had done God's will. And at the very least, her pa shall be happy to see her. Not to mention, she'd finally learn why Cole left New Callander.

"I shan't leave your side," he whispered.

"Thank you." She squeezed his hand, but withdrew as people began to exit the church. She may have convinced herself she could do this, but that didn't equate to its being easy.

She clasped her hands together and prayed the exact prayer she had recited when she had been petrified by that cougar. *Have not I commanded thee? Be strong and of a good courage; be not afraid, neither be thou dismayed; for the LORD they God [is] with thee withersoever thou goest.* She followed Mrs. Sherwood and Cole toward the parishioners who seemed to rush toward them. *God, You stayed with me in my last hour of need, please remain with me now.*

"Ma," Penny ran into her mother's outstretched arms. "I am all astonishment." Her friend leaned back out of their embrace to look at her mother. "P.J.," Penny called over her shoulder. "Ma's here." Her friend ran a hand over her mother's face as if she needed to touch her skin to prove her mother actually stood before her.

"Ma?" P.J. hugged his mother even tighter than his sister had, and the women's eyes misted. "How came you to be here?"

Cole stepped forward and shook hands with Blair McAllister, Penny's husband, his cousin, and one of his closest friends. "We brought her here to keep her safe. The Americans stationed at Fort George evacuated on Friday and ordered everything in their wake to be burnt. Unfortunately, her home was destroyed." He looked between Penny and P.J. "I'm sorry."

The horror that crossed their faces made her stomach hurt, and even though she wished nothing more than to remain silent and fade into a snow drift, she forced herself to speak on his behalf, "If it had been in Cole's power, please know he would have stopped them." She quieted when all eyes hit her.

"Jamie." Penny stepped forward. She braced herself. Perhaps she should no longer think of Penny as her friend. "I'm much obliged I'm sure, and so glad to see you all alive and well." Her friend held out her arms for a hug and she didn't hesitate to accept.

"Thank you," she murmured. "You cannot imagine how wonderful 'tis to see you again," she gushed, wishing desperately that Penny knew just how grateful she was for their friendship.

"Mrs. Sherwood," Fiona McAllister called out with glee as she rushed toward the widow with her husband, Lachlan McAllister, in tow. "I hadn't expected to see you here for Christmas. Penny, what a wonderful surprise for us all. However did you keep such a secret?"

"I knew not. I'm as surprised as you," Penny answered. "And my brother had no knowledge of her coming either."

"Oh, Mrs. Sherwood, my aunt always did have such lovely things to say about you." Fiona kissed Mrs. Sherwood on the cheek. "I hope you had a pleasant journey." She smiled in anticipation of the widow's answer,

but then her eyes fell upon Jamilyn,
and all her cheerfulness plummeted.

amilyn shivered. Fiona's expression had thrown a bucket of blood freezing cold liquid over her, worse than if she had plunged into the icy water of the Niagara River.

"I regret to say, my journey hadn't been planned in advance. 'Twas due entirely to necessity. However, I did enjoy a pleasant journey," Mrs. Sherwood's voice cut through the chilly air. "Thanks to Cole and Jamilyn." Violet took them both by the hand. "They saved my life."

Their protestations rambled over one another so fast their words rendered them unintelligible.

"Hush," Mrs. Sherwood scolded them with a grin. "I shall give credit where credit is due, and thanks to the two of you I'm here, alive. You saved me first from Doctor Blackstone, and then the fire, not to mention how you saved my beloved horses from being burnt alive."

"Oh, my." Penny's hand flew to her chest, and Fiona's face crumpled into shock.

"Pray tell, what happened," Lachlan said with soft compassion, even though his stature exhibited military authority.

"Aye," his cousin, Blair, echoed his words, and Mrs. Sherwood relayed the entire story to them with such praise that Jamilyn's cheeks grew more red with every word.

"I cannot thank you enough," Penny said through tears, and her brother reiterated her sentiment, as he shook hands with them.

"You need not thank us," Cole interposed.

"Jamilyn!" Her pa's voice stilled the crowd.

She laughed through the happiest of tears. She had barely ever heard her father raise his voice, and doubted anyone in attendance could recall such an occasion. "Pa." She hadn't expected to be overcome with emotion, but her heart swelled. His love shone brighter than the sun, and he hugged her tight for a long while.

"My darling." He cupped her face in his hands. "I cannot possibly express my delight in having you home."

The love in his eyes caused her to hold her tongue. She need not break his heart by mentioning her return was to be temporary. "Pa, I've missed you most ardently."

"I, as well, darling." He hugged her once more.

Parishioners patted her pa as they passed. Soon the crowd had thinned. "I must convey you home. We have much to discuss. And you must be tired from your travels." Her pa never released her as he clung to her arm. "Oh, God is good. He's answered my prayers. My baby home for Christmas."

She squeezed his arm and offered him a smile. "I must speak with a couple people first."

"Certainly, darling. I suppose we do indeed have the rest of the day, and the next, and the next," he laughed. "Don't mind me, I'm simply overjoyed beyond words."

"I love you, pa." She kissed his cheek.

"And I love you." He reluctantly released her.

She turned. Mrs. Sherwood stood surrounded by her children, but Fiona and Lachlan had left. "I missed my opportunity to apologize," she told Cole.

"We shall arrange another time."

She scoffed. "Perhaps you failed to notice the extent to which Fiona despises me."

"Perhaps we ought not to have surprised them. I shall speak with them. Fret not."

"Impossible." She met his eye, but before he could respond someone yelled his name.

"Cole!" His father hugged him, lifting him off his feet. A cry of pain exploded.

"Release him," she shouted. His father set him down. "Cole." She put her arm around his hunched over figure. "Please speak." With one hand on his thigh, he held up his index finger. The anguish on his face spoke volumes. "He suffers with cracked ribs," she told his horrified well-wishers.

Cole remained slumped in pain. Breathing hurt. Hence, speaking remained an impossibility. "Lean on me." Blair draped an arm around him for support. Jamilyn hobbled out of their way.

"Jamilyn, are you injured, as well?" her pa asked.

"I'm fine. I merely twisted my ankle. Cole however was kicked in the chest by a horse."

"Impossible," Blair blurted. "Cole, am I to believe that a mere several months away from your ranch and you've lost your savvy with horses?" He shot a glance at his cousin. "No need to strain yourself at the moment, but you must explain how you'd allow such an incident." He managed a grunt in response. "When you fare better of course."

"Cole, dear," his mother spoke softly. "We must take you home. You must rest. Blair would you be so kind as to help us see him home?"

"You need not ask," Blair assured her, then turned to his wife. "Penny—"

"We shall be fine. You tend to your cousin." Penny squeezed his shoulder. "Cole, do feel better. And thank you for bringing our mother to us safely." She gathered Blair's niece and sister, along with her mother and brother, and left them to their travels.

"I ought to take you home straight away, as well," Pastor West told Jamilyn. "We must tend to your ankle." Then he turned to them and said, "I shall pass the doctor's on our way, I shall stop in to have him examine Jamilyn's ankle and then I shall send him to your home straight away."

"Pa, 'tis most unnecessary," she argued. "Cole needs the doctor more than I. I'm fine."

"Nevertheless, as your father, I shall feel better once the doctor confirms it as such."

"As a mother, I agree. Thank you, Pastor," Cole's mother said. "The doctor shall lay all our fears to rest, I'm sure."

"Aye," his father interposed. "I feel awful, Cole. Had I known I never would have—"

"I know," he attempted to alleviate his father's guilt through clenched teeth. "We shall both be well in a few days." He smiled to encourage her. She responded with a wave as she

allowed her father to fuss over her as
he led her away.

How odd to see her leave and him
go in another direction. He had been
protecting her for months. Following
her back and forth to work. Hiding,
but always remaining close to her. And
now, the connection had been severed.

He had come to care for her, and
more than a friend. Something he most
definitely ought not to ever have
done. Hence, he'd view this separation
as an undeniably welcome one. He had
become overly involved, and
excessively close. That ended now.

*   *   *

Jamilyn sat before her vanity's
looking glass as she affixed her hair.
Four days had passed since she had
last seen Cole. Four *long* days. He had
said he'd visit her every day, and
yet, here she sat, day after day, and
he hadn't called once.

She pursed her lips. Perhaps his
suffering had prevented him. Or,
perhaps his work had been accomplished
and he no longer cared for her. She

had been his charge, and now that he had brought her home safely, his commission had been terminated. He was free to live his own life. A life that did not include her.

"Jamilyn, breakfast," her pa called.

"Coming," she answered, and rushed the remainder of her toilet.

Her pa smiled as she entered their dining room, that was only marginally larger than the table situated in the room's center with seating for eight. "I'm glad to see you walking better."

"Aye, you and the doctor were correct, resting these past few days has helped tremendously." She kissed his cheek, then as she passed the hearth in the corner, she pulled her skirt away from the fire. Pictures of family members in thick wooden frames looked down at her as she sat. "Thank you for the lovely breakfast," she told their cook. "You feed us as if we were royalty. Always such delicious meals."

"Aye," her pa agreed. "With food as delectable as this, I see no occasion for either of us to ever venture away from home."

"Oh, pa." She took his hand and squeezed it. "You know my reason for leaving."

"I do. And I disagreed with it then, and I shan't agree with it now."

"Let us enjoy this meal." She smiled at the cook, who excused herself from the room.

"Perhaps if you were to fall in love with someone local, that would provide an inducement to stay?"

She chuckled, "Pa. You must not set your hopes upon such unlikely outcomes." But her stomach knotted. She had indeed fallen for a local man—Cole. She'd never confide such nonsense to her pa though. To raise his hopes and then dash them would be reprehensible.

She'd never be good enough for Cole. Not with all of her failings. He only had to ask Lachlan and Fiona about those. Not that her failings even mattered, for he had no interest in her. She had been a means to an end, and her end had come. He obviously hadn't thought of her in the

way she had come to think of him. She
had been his charge. Period.

"That remains between God and
myself, and I place my whole trust in
God. He has heard my prayers, and as
the good book says in Matthew 7:7-7,
*Ask, and it shall be given you; seek,
and ye shall find; knock, and it shall
be opened unto you: For every one that
asketh receiveth; and he that seeketh
findeth; and to him that knocketh it
shall be opened.*"

"I cannot argue with that. Hence,
I propose we eat," she grinned.

He shook his head, but followed
her example.

"Perhaps some fresh air may
benefit me today," she mused. "We
neither of us have seen Cole since my
return. Do you not owe him money for
guarding me?"

"I believe I do, but he insists
otherwise."

"Wait, have you seen him?"

"Nay, but I have heard tell that
he is faring much better."

She concentrated on her food. His
refusal to accept money didn't prove
any devotion to her. He had told her

he had accepted the commission merely as an excuse to leave the Mohawk Valley. She must scold herself and not fall prey to such foolish thoughts. Why did she insist on renewing her attempts to prove he fancied her? He did not. She must accept that.

"Perhaps you ought to visit him anyhow. I assume you became friends during your ordeal and I need not remind you that the bedridden are our responsibility. Once more, Matthew has the answer in 25:35-40 *For I was hungry and you gave Me food; I was thirsty and you gave Me drink; I was a stranger and you took Me in; I was naked and you clothed Me; I was sick and you visited Me; I was in prison and you came to Me—*"

"Oh, pa. You are so fond of reciting scripture."

"I shan't deny it. 'Tis my calling in life."

"You're a good man, pa. And as such, I fear no man shall ever live up to you."

"Thank you for saying as much, 'tis indeed my principal endeavor to live as Jesus wished. And to know I have the love of my daughter, whom I adore, is a great blessing. And I am thankful every day for such a Godsend. But God shall bless you, as well, my child. I've prayed for such."

She forced her lips up. No doubt he had prayed endlessly for his prodigal daughter. And thus, she ought not refuse what little he asked of her. "If you wish me to visit Cole, I shall."

*   *   *

Cole sat looking out over their vast snow covered land, marveling at how different the fields appeared in any given season. His grandparents, Cait and Finnean Munro, started this ranch when they had immigrated from Scotland. They had passed the ranch down to his parents, and now they all considered it his turn to take the reins.

He sighed. His pun had failed to crack even the tiniest grin from him. This land ought to have belonged to his older brother.

"Cole," his grandmother, Cait, interrupted his thoughts. Which was just as well, they were once again about to head down a dark road. "You have a caller."

He attempted to stand, and for the first time since his arrival home, he finally did so with minimal aching. Soon, perhaps he would even forget to brace himself for pain. "Jamilyn?"

Her eyebrows slammed together. "Hello to you, as well, Cole."

"I shall leave you to visit." His grandmother smiled warmly at her as she rubbed her arm. "Please, do sit. And I could not help but notice you walked here. Hence, when you're about to leave, I shall call for the carriage."

She protested, "You need not—"

"'Tis my pleasure, dear, and you cannot refuse an old lady's wishes."

"I—" she sputtered.

He shot his grandmother a look. "Thank you." His grandmother's grin grew and she excused herself. "She takes enjoyment in making everyone bend to her will. And how can they not, when she guilts everyone with her

reference to herself as an old woman.
I dare say she may be advanced in
years, but in no other way." He
motioned for her to sit.

She dipped her chin, then sat in
the middle of one of the brown
cushioned sofas that faced each other
in front of the hearth.

He sat opposite her. "'Tis not
like you to be speechless." He smiled
as she busied herself with the olive
ribbon at her empire waist. Her shawl
and the pattern that ran over the
white fabric of her gown were
fashioned in the same green.

"I've come because my pa wished
it." She glanced at the books that
filled every shelf in the mahogany
bookcases that lined the room.

Now his eyebrows slammed
together. "Had I wrongfully assumed we
were friends?"

Her mouth gaped. "I believe that
question is one I ought to ask you."

"You believe me indifferent?" It
hurt she'd ever think that of him. But
on second thought, 'twould be for the
best.

"Aye. You have not come to see me these four days. Do you not remember your promise to visit every single day?" Her back straightened, a picture of indignation.

"I do indeed remember my words." He couldn't help but smile. "And I apologize. Please forgive me, I ought to have sent word to explain my absence. I see I didn't wrongfully assume our friendship, I wrongfully assumed you would hear word of my recovery and understand."

She leaned forward, the rigidity in her posture lessening. "Understand?"

"Aye. According to the doctor, I escaped with my life merely due to the horse being of the proper distance from me when it kicked. Apparently, had the horse been a wee bit closer I may have died instantly."

She gasped. "I'm sorry, Cole. Your injury is entirely my fault. I ought not to have insisted we save the horses. Your life is far more precious—"

"You cannot blame yourself. If anyone is to blame, 'tis I. I ought to

have anticipated the horses'
behavior—"

"Nonsense. You had not the time."

"Then I suppose since neither of
us shall allow the other to take the
blame, we must concede the horse to be
at fault."

She laughed. "I suppose you're
correct. Nonsensical horse. If only he
had seen reason and trusted us."

"Aye."

Her laughter lightened his heart.
He enjoyed seeing her mirth. She had
suffered enough. She needed happiness
in her life, more merriment and cheer.
And he hoped to offer her just that.
And only that. He could never offer
her more.

"Have you been in agony these
four days?"

"In a word, aye."

Her face fell into one of true
empathy.

"But despair not. The worst is
behind me. Thankfully my ribs are
intact and I shall heal from the
bruises that horse so kindly imparted
to me. But enough about me. I am most

glad to see you are able to walk once more."

"I believe *walk* may be a stretch. I hobble."

"But 'tis progress, is it not?"

"Aye. However, seeing as you know me, you may ascertain my impatience. I wish to be my old self, and this taxes on my nerves."

He chuckled, "How has your pa fared?"

"Just fine," she scoffed. "In fact, he's blissfully happy to have me home, and dotes on me excessively. He insisted I tell him everything—"

"And did you confide everything to him?"

"He merely wished to know of my daily endeavors. He never asked to know my deepest, inner thoughts. That honor belongs to you."

"I take offense at your insinuation that I'm meddlesome."

"I seriously doubt that."

"Fine," he grinned. "But please know my inquisitiveness is due to caring." She quieted, and he wished to kick himself. He shan't give her the impression he harbored amorous feelings for her. "I cannot help but care. Perhaps you may not have known, but my brother regarded you rather highly."

"I most certainly knew nothing of the sort."

He dipped his chin. He hadn't wished to reveal anything about his brother, but to exit this potentially volatile situation, a fragment of revelation was a mere pittance. "'Tis true. Hence, in devotion to his memory, or perhaps to continue his legacy, I feel a certain obligation toward you." She sat motionless. He ought to kick himself again. That horse must have knocked something loose in his brain.

"I understand," she croaked.

Clearly, she did not. "This is another reason why I shan't stay. I cannot live in the past. And since my return, my family has talked of nothing but. They are rather misguided in their attempt to convince me to stay," he babbled. Perhaps if enough words escaped his lips, some of them would finally make sense. "Every conversation veers to me accepting ownership of the ranch."

"You cannot fault them. Surely, you must understand their motive. You're their only heir."

"I shan't fault you for such a statement, but aye, I do fault them. They, who know, and ought to understand my reason." He ground his teeth. "Please understand, I cannot merely assume my brother's life. A life, he's no longer able to live due to me."

"Due to you? Please, elaborate."

"You must know that I cannot afford to laugh, the action pains me. However, I do applaud your clever attempt to goad me into revealing the thoughts of my inner mind. But, perhaps you've forgotten our agreement. You must make amends first."

She blew out a breath. "I suppose 'tis only fair you hold me to our agreement. But you must have seen Fiona. If looks could cause harm I shan't be sitting here now."

"Surely, you must know she shan't harm you."

"Be that as it may, my task shan't be an easy one."

"Nay, I dare say it shan't. You do still plan to apologize though?"

"Aye. And seeing as I have been successful in coming to see you, I shan't have any excuse not to visit Fiona and Lachlan."

"When then do I have until before I must tell you what you long to know?"

"My curiosity cannot wait until church on Sunday. Hence, I shall attempt to visit the McAllisters on the morrow."

He swallowed the lump in his throat. He dearly wished her to make amends. But he certainly did not wish to confide in her about his brother. "Perhaps you ought not apologize."

"Cole, I cannot believe you." She grimaced. "I shall apologize, for 'tis the right thing to do. However, knowing you must share something you'd rather not, has now added more sugar to the tea."

"I'm glad." He chuckled. "But speaking of tea, would you care for a cup?"

"Thank you, nay." She stood. "I must away to prepare for tomorrow."

"As you wish." He rose and took her hand. "All joking aside, I shall pray all goes well."

"I do indeed appreciate any and all prayers."

Her eyes held his. And how long they remained standing holding hands he knew not. "Shall I accompany you tomorrow?" He truly did wish to support her. To stand beside her. To ease her burdens.

"Nay. I shan't impose."

"'Tis not an imposition if I offered."

She shook her head. "You must rest. Christmas is a mere week away. You must recover. And besides, it shall offer you more time to compose your narrative."

He laughed. "I see I shall need to admit defeat and ready myself."

"I do expect the entire story."

"Even if knowing all may change everything?"

She stared at him a long moment. "Aye, even then. You must unburden yourself. And as your friend, I shall cope with whatever you lay at my feet." At least she had referred to herself as his *friend,* for she was soon to learn why they could never be more.

*   *   *

Jamilyn wrung her hands. If 'tweren't for her ankle she'd have paced in front of Lachlan and Fiona's one and a half story, stone home enough to rid their entire property of snow.

"Jamilyn?" Her head jerked to see Lachlan storm toward her.

"Lachlan" Jamilyn blurted, knowing her lame utterance stood insufficient. She had no right to be here on his land given her past behavior. She was as unwelcome as a snow storm.

"Why have you come?" He stared with hardened features. Not at all the face of the man she remembered. Obviously, he now cared nothing for her. Their friendship was no more.

But she shan't turn tail and run. She stood straighter. "I'm here to apologize."

He crossed his arms, careful not to bother the area where he had been shot. "I'm listening."

She hadn't expected a warm welcome. In fact, she was somewhat surprised at his tolerance in providing her an audience at all. But she had prayed for such an opportunity. And squander it, she most definitely shan't. "I am truly sorry for my actions toward you and Fiona. I regret them in their entirety. I am deeply ashamed, and sorry for the hurt I caused. I was selfish and misguided. You were my friend, and I failed to behave as one toward you. I know I caused you immense pain. Not only you, but Fiona."

He sucked in a long, deep breath. She hadn't been eloquent. Her words sprayed in a jumbled mess. She must state more clearly her deepest reasons for her regret. "You always showed me great compassion. The likes of a true friend, such as yourself, there never was. I confused your friendship with love. I believed we were meant to be together. Please know, I realize that to be utter foolishness now. But unfortunately, I did not then. I believed you to be the only man who would ever know my history and yet still love me. I believed that if you slipped away, all my dreams of happiness and marriage would be gone forever, as well."

"And now you think differently?"

"Indeed I do. You love Fiona and she loves you. She is who you are meant to be with. She is the one who holds your heart. And I am happy for you both, and I wish you every felicitation and blessing in the world. I ought not to have ever attempted to put your relationship asunder. "

"Thank you for saying as much, and for your explanation. Cole has interceded on your behalf, and hence, I am apt to believe you." His arms fell to his sides. "And as you have confessed, so too shall I. I was most sorry to lose your friendship."

His words pierced her heart. She had deeply damaged the friendship of a most loyal and compassionate friend. Her oldest and dearest one, to be exact. Tears misted behind her eyes. She had been completely ridiculous and nonsensical. "God knows I cannot be more sorry. I understand if you and Fiona never wish to speak with me again. I am just grateful you allowed me to unburden myself so I may repent for my misdeeds."

"It shall take time to make amends fully, but if, as Cole asserts, you are truly sorry, and have changed, I see not why we cannot mend our friendship over time."

She wished to drop to her knees and thank God. Lachlan had extended her an olive branch, and 'twas all due to Him, and Cole. "You are all goodness. Thank you. I know I don't deserve such treatment, but I appreciate this new occasion to obtain both your friendship and Fiona's. And if it pleases you, I would like very much to apologize to her, as well."

"I think that a capital idea. Please, come inside." He held out his arm to offer her aid as they cautiously stepped through the snow. Always the gentleman, for despite his own wound, he knew of her injured ankle. "I know how much you've suffered in life. Just as I knew your behavior didn't reflect the friend I had always known. I prayed for you. I never gave up hope that you'd see the light. Hence, I must confess, I had a hand in you becoming the cook at Fort George, and assuring Cole was welcome there."

Her jaw dropped. After all she had done. The man beside her had truly been sent from God. "I didn't deserve your kindness."

"Your pa and Cole would beg to differ. And if I may be so bold as to ask, do you believe that perhaps you may find happiness with Cole?"

"Cole?" she choked.

"Aye. You are friends, are you not?"

"We are, but—"

"He followed you into enemy territory. He placed himself in danger of death to protect you."

"He had other reasons. He's not in love with me. I fear you've misread the situation. But fear not, I shan't ever hurt you or Fiona again. I hold your marriage in sanctity. You mustn't fret over my not having a beau, or being courted, or my unmarried status."

"After your apology, we shan't. But perhaps you ought to readdress your relationship with Cole."

"Forgive me, I know I have been wrong in countless ways, but in this, you must believe me to be correct. He does not feel for me in the way a husband ought. He merely feels a sense of obligation and duty toward me."

"I shan't argue further, for we've arrived, and I do wish you to make peace with Fiona." He opened their wooden door and motioned her in. "Fiona," he called. "We have a visitor."

She swallowed a lungful of air. Her conversation with Lachlan had afforded better results than expected.

But Fiona was a different kettle of fish. They had not the history. And she knew not what to expect. Perhaps his wife would even dissuade him.

"Bring our guest in," Fiona's cheerful voice called from the kitchen. "I've just baked biscuits."

He stepped forward with an enormous grin. She grabbed his arm. "Perhaps you ought to warn Fiona of my presence. I shan't wish to upset her."

He studied her a moment. "As you wish. I shan't be but a moment. Do sit." He motioned to the drawing room.

Her feet however, had frozen themselves to the floorboards. But that was just as well, given that she'd never be able to relax anyhow. And the slight pain in her ankle provided her with a distraction. However, the distraction proved fleeting, as hushed voices carried themselves into the hall. Fiona's displeasure was evident. Perhaps she ought to leave. She glanced at the door.

Nay. She must say what she had come to say. She must apologize—for herself, for Lachlan and Fiona, and for Cole. That man needed her help. Hence, come what may, she must face Fiona, so she could help him. *God, be with me.*

"Do come in," Lachlan said from the doorway.

With mashed lips, she stepped forth. "Fiona, I beg your pardon for the intrusion. But I've come to apologize. And I thank you profusely for allowing me the opportunity to do so," she rambled, determined to issue her apology before anything prevented her. "I am most ashamed of my behavior toward you. My thoughts and actions were misguided and hurtful. I believed—"

"Lachlan has informed me of the particulars."

Fiona's curt manner gave her pause, but then she rallied, "My reasons matter not. I behaved deplorably and I shall remain forever sorry. I caused you and Lachlan needless pain. I shall understand if you despise me, and wish me away. But knowing Lachlan loves you, offers me hope. He is all good, and hence, I believe him incapable of loving anyone unlike himself. To now think of how I treated you, I am repulsed. I cannot even comprehend my own behavior. Please believe in my reform. I am truly repentant. And God-willing I shall live out my days as a better person."

Fiona opened her mouth to speak, but she couldn't bear any ill tidings and blurted, "I've come with a peace offering. I believe this belongs to you." She held forth a satchel. "Doctor Blackstone presented this to me as a gift. He apparently found it under a floor board in his home, and I believe his home once belonged to you. Hence, I believe this piece of jewelry to be yours. And I do so wish to return it to its rightful owner, as I'm certain a gold necklace with such a fine cross medallion must be a family heirloom and of great value to you."

Tears fell as Fiona pulled out the delicate chain. "In my rush to flee, I must have somehow left this behind. 'Tis more dear to me than you know. Thank you."

"Please, you must not thank me. I am merely doing that which is right. I'm only grateful I have the opportunity to make amends. If Doctor Blackstone was sorry for the harm he caused, he died before he had the opportunity."

"Edgar is gone," Fiona sputtered. She nodded. "I must sit." Lachlan helped her to a chair at the kitchen table.

"You're with child," she spat. Then slammed her palm over her lips. "How impertinent of me, I apologize. But I am most happy for you both. I truly wish you all the joy this world has to offer. God has blessed you, and I know of no other two people who deserve it more. And I shall guard your secret until you make your situation known."

"Thank you." Fiona rubbed a hand over their baby. "We were waiting to announce our blessing on Christmas."

"What a gift that shall be for your family and friends. Truly, I am happy for you."

"Thank you for saying as much, and for your apology. I know it must not have been easy," Fiona said.

Her kindness stabbed. How could she ever have hurt such a lovely person? Never again. The new her would always strive to live as Jesus had. "I do hope and pray that in time we may meet as acquaintances, and not enemies."

"I dare say, we may soon meet as friends," Lachlan interposed. "Cole wishes nothing less."

"Is Cole courting you?" Fiona asked.

"Nay," she adamantly replied. "We're friends. Just two people helping one another."

"He is a good man," Lachlan pronounced.

"I shan't argue with that," she agreed. "But again, we are but only friends."

They exchanged a look, that caused her much apprehension. "I can see from your disparaging looks, and from your insistence of our relationship, that you do not believe me. And I suppose I cannot be affronted given my past behavior, but truly I tell you that as of this moment, we are no more than friends. And I do so wish you to believe me. For I have come to tell nothing but truths."

"Our intention was never to imply that you had lied," Fiona blurted. "We merely think your relationship may be worth pursuing. Do you not agree with us?"

"I—um—well—I hadn't—that is to say—I—um—"

"Let us speak no more of this," Lachlan interjected. "But please, do consider it."

She dipped her chin.

*   *   *

Jamilyn thought of nothing else but Fiona and Lachlan's words. They wished her to consider a relationship with Cole. Even though Cole was Blair's cousin, and Blair was Lachlan's cousin, so for all intents and purposes they were family. They must truly have forgiven her, or why else would they desire her to marry one of Lachlan's closest friends.

However she turned it about in her head, the fact remained that they would never wish her to marry Cole unless they thought her good enough. And this had caused her to cry, on several occasions. The relief, the breaking of her remorseful chains, the knowledge that her distress had come to end, had filled her with such an overwhelming sense of gratitude. She knew she owed her thanks to God. But she would forever be indebted to Cole, as well, who had impelled her to act.

"Jamilyn, breakfast," her pa called.

A laugh escaped her lips. She had been home less than a week and simply living in this house with her pa provided such deep comfort. How had she ever left? Her pa was dearer to her than anyone. "Pa," she began when she had entered their dining room. "I could not speak yesterday when I returned home, I was so overwrought with emotion, but I'd like to speak to you now, if you've the time."

"I always have time for you, darling." He pulled her out a chair.

"My visit with Lachlan and Fiona went well. I apologized, and I believe they forgave me."

"My prayers were answered." He clasped his hands together. "I cannot tell you how light and happy my heart is at this moment. But I must ask, have you forgiven yourself?"

She stilled. "I haven't given that thought any consideration."

"You ought to. God wishes us to love Him, but also to love our neighbours as ourselves. But you cannot do that, if you do not forgive yourself, and love yourself once more."

She stared blankly. "I know your words to be correct, but pa how can I? I was horrible."

"Precisely. You *were*. You are no longer the same person you were then. And you've made amends. You've apologized. You've repented. You're truly sorry. You cannot punish yourself forevermore."

His words struck her like a clump of ice falling off the church roof. "I shall think upon it."

"Good. For I know before long you shall see I'm correct and begin to live your life as you ought. You have your entire life ahead of you. Perhaps even marriage and children in your future." He bumped her with his elbow several times, his smile wider than the room. "Not to boast, but I shall be an excellent grandpa. I promise."

She laughed, "I've no doubt. But pa, you've put the cart before the horse. I haven't even a beau."

"Minutiae."

She chuckled. "I hardly believe having a man fall madly in love with me a trivial detail."

"Have you not considered Cole?"

"Cole?" She nearly fell off her chair. "Did you speak with Lachlan and Fiona?" He shook his head. "They offered the same suggestion."

"Great minds think alike."

"Pa, you ought to watch yourself. Boasting of being an excellent grandpa and now having a great mind, whatever shall the Lord think?"

"The Lord knows I am giddy with happiness. My daughter home and forgiven."

She reached over and squeezed his hand. "You have given me much to ponder. But pa, you must know, Cole is not in love with me. I'm sorry to disappoint you, but we are merely friends."

"If you say so." He squeezed her hand back. "But let us eat, we shan't be forgiven if we allow this food to spoil."

"I dare say, you are correct." She ate, but her mind raced. She knew her pa to always be correct in matters such as these. Hence, she must forgive herself. Although she knew not how or when.

But, to think of Cole as a potential suitor? He clearly had no intentions to proclaim that title. However, one thing he must proclaim, was his secret about his brother. She had made amends, and hence, he now must confide in her.

*　　*　　*

Cole stared at the flames dancing in the hearth. He had done nothing but rest since his arrival home. And although that did indeed help his recovery, he wished it to be tomorrow when he'd be able to venture outdoors for a change of scenery at church.

"Cole." His mother swept into the sundrenched parlor accented in red draperies, a wool carpet, and upholstered chairs and chaises to match. "You have a caller."

"Thank you," Jamilyn said to his mother.

"You're welcome. Enjoy your visit," his mother sang herself out of the room.

Jamilyn passed the table in the center of the room and seated herself on the opposite side of the hearth in another fireside wing chair. "Have you recovered much?"

"Aye. More and more every day. Soon I shan't even caution myself not to bend over, and I shan't cringe before I cough, sneeze, or laugh. And how do you fare?"

"Much better, as well. I believe I shall be fully healed by Christmas."

"I'm happy for you. I believe I may need a wee bit longer. Perhaps by the new year."

"Wonderful. We shall usher in the new year as new people."

"I know not about that."

"Then I'm happy to know for the both of us."

"My, you do indeed talk with noted cheerfulness this day. To what do we owe this change?"

She grinned, but something mischievous hid behind it. "I visited Lachlan and Fiona yesterday."

"Oh, Jamilyn, I'm proud of you. Did I not tell you how amazingly courageous you are."

"I'm unsure of the accuracy of such a declaration, but you offered me the exact inducement I needed, and so I thank you. I feel lighter, as if a mighty weight has been lifted from me. And Lachlan and Fiona were gracious and forgiving. And I know I owe you more thanks for interceding on my behalf."

"You're most welcome." He wished to twirl her about the room. "This calls for a celebration. I shall ring the bell."

"Nay, please." She grew serious. "As thrilled as I am. You must realize that I must now insist—"

"That I confide in you?"

She nodded. "You promised, and I know you to be an honest gentleman who ought never to disappoint."

He put his hands together as if in prayer and banged them several times on his lips. "Aye. A promise is a promise. But before I do tell all, please reconsider what I'm about to reveal. You cannot unhear it once 'tis pronounced. Perhaps you may wish to reconsider?"

"I'm afraid I cannot, for I believe that in the telling you may overcome this burden that rests with such heaviness upon you, just as I did before making amends. Please know my intention is not to torture you, but to help. And I truly believe this shall help."

He looked up the length of the hearth that reached the ceiling. "I fail to see how. If anything, this

shall add greatly to my unhappiness.
Please, do reconsider. I beg you."

"I'm sorry."

He stared at her a long time,
then finally blurted, "Fine. I cannot
break my promise. If you wish to know
how my brother was killed, how I
killed my brother, then so be it."

amilyn's voice sang through the parlor with steadfast conviction, "I am certain you could not have purposely killed your brother, Cole."

"My negligence and steadfast determination did." He fretted with irritation and unease as she sat calmly awaiting his narrative.

"I shall judge that for myself once I know all."

He raked a hand through his hair. This was it. The moment she'd know all. After this, their friendship would forevermore be changed. If only he knew of another way to avoid telling her. He thought hard, but nothing manifested itself.

"Do take all the time you need. I shall wait. I've no prior commitments." She settled comfortably into her chair.

"Before I begin, I must implore you to remain my friend after all is said and done."

"Cole, I cannot believe anything you are about to say shall alter our friendship. Thus, I implore you to begin. Please."

He looked away from her and into the fire. "On the day of my brother's death, he and I had been teasing each other incessantly. He had been speaking so forlornly though at times, that in retrospect, 'tis as if somehow he knew the end of his life had come.

I've tried hard to forget that day and remember him in happier times, hence you must bear with me as my memory of that day is broken. "

"I shan't mind. I'm merely thankful you're to finally confide in me."

She may not think as such for long. "I cannot remember the particulars of how we arrived at our decision to race to the top of a mountain that day, but as we stood at the bottom, my brother confronted me about the unrequited feelings I held for a certain lady he knew."

She cried out, "I knew not that you loved someone."

"I had not made my feelings known to her. Hence, 'twas only my brother, Blair, and Lachlan who possessed any knowledge of it."

"You're speaking in the past tense."

"I am." He sat in awe of her keen mind. "For I can no longer love her. But, let us not digress. My brother chose that moment, at the foot of the mountain, to inform me that he too loved the same woman."

"Nay," she gasped.

"Aye. And I held no prior knowledge, not even an inkling. Later, I asked Blair, and Lachlan, and they too had never heard him profess any intentions toward her. But as 'twere, there we stood knowing one of us must walk away from this lady and allow the other to pursue her."

"But neither of you walked away, correct?"

"Correct. But how I wish every second of every minute that I had."

"You couldn't have known," she cooed.

"I ought not to have accepted his challenge. I ought to have formulated another way for us to decide who'd court her."

Haughtily, she crossed her arms and said, "Or you ought to have allowed her to decide."

"Not possible." He grimaced. "Can you not imagine if she were to have married one of us knowing the other had been in love with her? How awkward and ill-at-ease we'd all be. The other brother eternally miserable. Nay. This had to be decided between us."

"Perhaps there may have been a way to discern her feelings without revealing yours?"

"Unfortunately, such an idea had not occurred to me then. How I regret my thinking. I ought to have devised another plan."

"Oh, Cole. I apologize. I did not intend to—"

"I know. And fret not. 'Tis I who must forevermore rebuke myself for how I behaved." Indeed, the pain of that day rested enormously heavy on his chest. Even before he had been kicked by that horse the task of breathing had taxed him every time his brother flashed into his mind.

"And how exactly did you behave?"

"My brother challenged me to a competition, and I accepted."

"Seems a natural circumstance for many brothers to find themselves in."

"Aye, but in this competition, a significant prize greeted the victor. You see, the first one to race to the top of the mountain, claimed the honor of courting the lady. And hence, as we raced our horses, my mind lay solely focused on competing, and winning. I failed to even notice how much of the race I rode alone. Once I reached the top, I rejoiced in my victory, and applauded myself. That is, until a considerable amount of time passed and my brother never appeared. I searched and searched, but never found him, or his horse. To this day, I know not where their bodies lay."

"Oh, Cole. I'm truly sorry." Her eyes were filled with as many tears as his. "But I knew your brother's death could never have been your fault."

He jumped to his feet, pain shot through his chest, but he cared not. "My brother's death was most certainly my fault. If I hadn't agreed—"

"Your brother suggested the race. Do you blame him?"

"Nay."

"Then you shan't blame yourself. Neither of you are to blame. His death, as awful and untimely as 'twas, happened by accident. You shan't carry guilt from that day." She leaned forward, full of zeal, "Mourn his loss. Miss him. Pray for him to be with Jesus. But never blame yourself, or ruin your life living it in guilt.

His death was an accident, not intentional. As you said, if you'd have known you never would have agreed."

He remained silent a long while, then spoke just above a whisper, "If I hadn't loved this woman with every fiber of my being, perhaps he'd still be alive. My mind lay solely focused on her. And I cannot forgive myself for that. I ought to have considered my brother, not merely my own selfish desires."

Now she sat in silent contemplation. But, when she spoke, her reproach hit him hard, "If you wish to avoid any further *selfishness,* then I suggest you forgive yourself. For, as I see it, you're behaving absolutely selfishly now."

He gaped. "How?"

"Your family desires you to inherit the ranch, and you refuse. Your decision hurts them. You must know as much. Here you sit licking your wounds, whilst they fret about the future of the ranch, and you. If you learn to focus on them, instead of yourself, you shall see the situation differently."

He crossed his arms. Perhaps her words were sensical, but she had ruffled his feathers, and he sat in a huff. "I cannot simply take what ought to have belonged to my brother. And I shan't ever make my feelings known to the lady, for I believe she belongs to my brother, and I shan't ever inherit the ranch, for that ought to have been his, as well."

"Listen to me. This lady, no more belongs to your brother, than to you, especially given how both of you never made your intentions known. And as for the ranch, aye, your brother ought to have inherited it had he lived, but that is not the present state. Your family knows this. You must accept this. He is gone. You are here. Through no fault of your own. 'Tis now incumbent upon you to take the lead for your family. 'Tis your duty."

Her heart beat rapidly. She hadn't held any thoughts in. He had always appreciated her forthrightness. But in this moment it appeared he did not. "Are you satisfied that I've confided in you?" his tone sailed even.

"Aye. Thank you." But his tone had screamed that he had endured enough. "Oh, look at the time. I cannot believe I've trespassed on your hospitality this long. Forgive me. I shall see you at church on the morrow?" He dipped his chin. She knew she had given him a mouthful and hence much to think on. "Until tomorrow then." She rose. "Nay, please sit. I can see myself out. And thank you once more for keeping your promise to confide in me. You are a righteous man." With that, she left before he could utter a rebuke.

How exactly she returned home she knew not. Her body had gone through the motions, but her mind had been tangled in the mystery of who Cole had loved. And in all likelihood, still loved.

Her stomach hurt with the thought of him in love with another woman. Although, as much as it pained her, this time, she shan't stand in the way of true love. She had changed, and she'd prove it. He was her dearest friend, and if he loved someone, she'd help him find happiness with her. She only needed to discover this woman's identity.

*   *   *

Jamilyn hurried to church for the last Sunday service before Christmas Eve on Friday. Cole had said both Blair and Lachlan knew who he had been in love with. Hence, she must speak with them.

"Jamilyn," Mrs. Sherwood bounded down the church steps and straight for her. "I cannot tell you how happy I am to be among my children."

"'Tis wonderful. I'm so glad." They hugged.

"And you're walking much better."

"Thank you. I'm certain a few more days shall set me right."

Mrs. Sherwood held onto her arm tight and pulled her to the side. "I have the most wonderful news. And I know I can trust you to keep our secret," she whispered. "I'm to be a grandmother."

She smiled. "Oh, what a Christmas blessing."

"I couldn't agree more." Her eyes shone with merriment and she exuded a true vivaciousness. "And I must thank you once more for bringing me here. Imagine, now I shall be present for every moment of this baby's life."

She squeezed her arm. "You're most welcome." And she was most relieved that Violet's uprooting had resolved itself in such an advantageous way. Her own return had proven rather pleasing, as well. She had made amends, and had started on her journey to forgive herself. The only one still not healed was Cole. But she would see to that. "Have Blair and Penny come?"

"Aye, they're in the church. Penny feels most unwell, but I pray that passes soon as is usual for most women. Although, the way Blair dotes on her. Be still, my beating heart."

"He is a good man, and she is most fortunate to have wed him."

"Aye. And now we must see you wed."

She fumbled several incoherent words, causing Violet to cackle.

"There, there dear. Perhaps I shall leave my matchmaking until after Christmas?"

She laughed. "If that pleases you, I shan't stand in the way of your happiness." Nor would she with Blair or Lachlan. Blair was understandably preoccupied with his wife and unborn baby, as was Lachlan. Perhaps she hadn't thought her plan through enough. Her prying about Cole may be unwelcome. And, it may appear most odd if she were to walk up to either of the men and demand they tell her who Cole loved.

Perhaps, she ought to winkle the information from the source. Cole had confirmed he'd be at church.

"Cole," Mrs. Sherwood called.

Her eyes locked with his. She knew not when her feelings had developed for him, but the fretful beating of her heart confirmed it. Somewhere along the way, she had fallen deeply in love with him. She no longer saw him as a mere friend. She saw her future happiness, completely and irrevocably, tied to him.

"Ladies." He tipped his rabbit-felt top hat.

Mrs. Sherwood released her arm and strode toward him. "You have much improved. I'm glad."

"Thank you. And you are well I hope?" he inquired.

She winked at her. "Much better than well, thank you. But, excuse me, I have tarried far too long, my family must wonder at my whereabouts. I shall speak with you both later?"

"Certainly," she replied, and he agreed.

"Wonderful." Violet squeezed both of their hands, then strode into the church, as if she were the sun.

"'Tis most pleasing to see her happy," he commented.

"I am utterly relieved. Remember how she fought us? I thank God for her merriment."

"Aye. My family is displeased with me enough. Imagine how much more so they'd be if I had tortured a poor, old woman."

She ought to have laughed, but she couldn't. "I'm sorry to hear of your family's displeasure. But I do agree with them. I believe you ought to inherit the ranch. You love horses. You love this town. All of your family and friends reside here. I understand your reasoning, but I wholly disagree with you. Your brother is gone, through no fault of your own, and you are here. I believe it to be your duty."

"Allow me to reiterate, I cannot in good conscience simply assume my brother's life."

"You're not assuming his life, you're living your own. We none of us understand God's will in everything."

He shook his head. "I cannot believe I'm supposed to own the ranch. And I certainly cannot court the woman my brother loved."

"But you loved her, as well."

"Aye, but my brother can no longer fight for her." Regret creased his forehead.

"Perhaps that is as 'twas meant to be." He stared at her hard. His anger evident and escalating. But she would not relent. She must break through to him. "Your brother wouldn't wish this life of exile for you."

He scoffed. "I dare say he wouldn't wish me in his rightful place."

"That is precisely what your guilt blocks you from understanding. You're here. Hence, you belong here. For whatever reason, he does not anymore. 'Tis your rightful place now."

"You misconstrue the situation," he hissed. His voice low, only due to the fact they stood near the church. She knew he seethed in torment at what he wished not to hear.

She squared her shoulders. "I think not."

"Perhaps you wouldn't think as such if you knew you were the woman my brother loved, the one he wished to marry and make mistress of his ranch." Whatever she had been about to counter with fell from her thoughts. "That ought to have been your life, and now it never shall."

She continued to stare. Then her mind awoke and she blurted, "But that would mean—"

He grimaced and rushed out, "Please, forget my words, they were spoken in the haste of anger." His eyes pierced her as he dipped a slight bow, then strode into the church.

She stood frozen in the cold white snow, and mumbled to herself, *that would mean you loved me.* Loved, as in the past tense, seeing as he had sworn to himself never to court her. Tears gushed, and she ran home.

*   *   *

Jamilyn heard the front door open. She rose from the sofa in their parlor and wiped profusely at her eyes. She had completely lost track of time. Church must have ended a while ago. She ought to have prepared herself.

"Jamilyn," her pa called. "I did not see you in church, are you unwell?"

"Aye, pa." She straightened her dress and attempted to tidy her hair.

317

Her pa stopped as he entered the room, then approached her slowly. "You've been crying." He handed her his handkerchief. "Please, sit. Do tell me why." She fumbled with the embroidered cloth. "Please, 'tis always helpful to unburden yourself, and I shan't judge or be cross. I only ever wish to help."

Such a dear pa. Her eyes stung with fresh tears. "Oh, pa." She threw herself into his arms and wept.

He held her tight. When the worst of her tears had flowed, he cooed, "Hush, my dear. Come, let's sit. Unburden yourself."

"Oh, pa." She dried her eyes. "I received the most horrid news before church. I have been overcome with emotion ever since."

He sat beside her. "What has happened?"

"I have fallen in love with a man, pa," she blurted.

An amused smile lit his face. "'Tis a most natural predicament that ought not to provoke tears." He tucked a strand of her hair behind her ear.

"Oh, but pa, you haven't heard all."

"'Tis not with a married man?" he grew serious.

"Nay, pa, Never."

"Then, why cry? Is this man in love with someone else?"

When she thought he had been, she had remained strong. She had thought of it as a proper penance. A chance to prove to God and everyone that she had truly changed. She had prepared herself to be happy for him and to help him at the expense of herself. But now, everything had changed.

"Worse." She pulled the handkerchief in all different directions. Then, her words came as a flood, "He can never love me because his deceased brother loved me. And there was a competition to see who ought to court me, but that is when his brother died, and now the living brother refuses to accept his new life. And he shall never consider courting me because of his brother dying in the midst of the competition, and pa, the entire situation is a complete mess. I had been attempting

to help, but I fear I've made matters
worse, and now the man I love shan't
ever talk to me again. He never meant
to reveal any of this to me. I don't
think anyone knows. Although, everyone
knows the brother died, but not the
other parts. And he's angry—"

"Slow down, please. I fail to
understand."

"Pa," she sobbed. "'Tis Cole."

"Cole Munro?"

She nodded.

"You're in love with Cole. And he
loves you, as well?"

"Aye. Nay. He did. But he cannot
now that his brother has died."

"Is this why he refuses to
inherit his family's ranch?"

"He's determined not to obtain
anything that ought to have belonged
to his brother."

"There, there. Dry your tears. We
shall convince him to see reason."

"I see not how, pa. His family
has spoken with him ad nauseum."

"Fret not, my dear. Please.
Saturday is Christmas. 'Tis the time
for miracles." He rose. "I shall send
in some tea. But promise me you shan't

cry any longer, for I must away for the afternoon."

"I shall make a valiant attempt." She smiled. "You need not trouble yourself where I am concerned. I shall pray and lay my problems in God's hands."

He kissed the top of her head. "So I *have* taught you something."

"Everything. And thank you, pa." He left and she knew she had cheered him. She, however, still felt as if her heart had been on fire and now a hole lay in the middle of her chest.

*   *   *

Cole had been relieved not to have seen Jamilyn in church. But the guilt of knowing their conversation had been the cause of her not entering the house of God had seared him. And he couldn't be the reason she didn't attend church tomorrow for Christmas Eve.

But how would he face her after what he had revealed? How foolish to confide that his brother had loved her. Now, she knew he had loved her, as well. Perhaps he could convince her his feelings were in the past and he no longer harbored any intentions toward her. Then, they could remain friends.

Not possible. She'd never believe it to be true. Not after he had followed her to Upper Canada to guard her. She had to know his feelings were stronger than they had ever been. He had risked his life for her. He'd die for her if need be.

He clasped his hands together, closed his eyes tight, and prayed, just as he had done ever since his brother had died. He begged Mary to intercede on his behalf to Jesus and untie these knots. He knew not of any possible end to this mess that would result in everyone's happiness. How could any of this be resolved favorably? His brother was dead.

And yet, the words from Proverbs that he had heard often in church rang through his mind, *Trust in the Lord with all thine heart; And lean not unto thine own understanding. In all thy ways acknowledge Him, And He shall direct thy paths.*

He took a deep breath. He must face Jamilyn. He had ruined his brother's life, he wouldn't devastate hers, as well. He strode to the front vestibule and donned his great coat and hat. "I need some exercise," he told a maid, who had happened to walk by. "Please, inform my family for me." She dipped a curtsey. "Thank you." He threw the door open and inhaled the fresh, crisp air that only existed this time of year.

He had been cooped up in the house for far too long. The only trace of happiness he felt however was when he realized walking didn't hurt as much as it had. He was recovering. And he thanked God. Now, he needed to set his mind on convincing Jamilyn he no longer loved her.

"Cole," his name blew through the breeze. He looked up to see Pastor West hurrying toward him. "I was on my way to your house to speak with you."

He stopped. "Shall we return? I shan't wish to keep you out in this cold."

"Nay. Thank you. But if you shall permit me the intrusion, I desire you to accompany me."

"If you wish." He followed the pastor. "Is this of an urgent matter?"

"Aye. But fret not. All is as it ought to be."

Most peculiar. He walked in quiet contemplation, all the while wondering where exactly the pastor led him. Had she told her father all, and now he sought to lecture him in private, or perhaps he led him to her in an attempt to reconcile them. "May I know our destination?"

"All in good time."

Most mysterious. And aggravating. Ready to confront Jamilyn, he most certainly was not. He had yet to formulate a plan or even think of a way to portray himself so she would misconstrue his feelings and believe he no longer cared.

"We've arrived," Pastor West cheered to himself.

He did not join in the merriment. "'Tis the oldest barn on our property. It has fallen into much disrepair and is no longer in use. " He regarded the dilapidating building. He could not step into his brother's life, but how he itched to bring this structure back to its former glory.

"Precisely why we've come." A smile licked his lips.

Most odd. And for a pastor, extremely unnerving . "Pastor West, I must demand to know why you've summoned me hence?"

"After careful consideration, involving many minds, and four days, we have finally executed a plan to help you, nay save you—"

"Save me? I wasn't aware I needed to be saved." He planted his feet firmly in the snow. Perhaps the pastor was the one who stood in need of saving, and h had just unwittingly followed a mad man about his property. "Pray tell me specifically to what do you speak of?"

He shook his head. "I shan't, for I shall show you."

"Fine." He knew he was in no danger with the pastor, even though he had never witnessed the man behave in such a bizarre fashion. "Please, lead on."

"Before I do, I must warn you—"

"Whatever you are to show me, I assure you I shan't pale." He crossed his arms, and despite everything, he wished Jamilyn was present, for perhaps she could explain her father.

"Very well then. I shall leave you to enter the barn alone." He touched his forearm. "Merry Christmas."

"Merry Christmas, to you, as well." Baffled, he watched the man walk away. Then, he turned to face the crumbling building. He could not fathom any possible reason to enter. But the pastor had insisted, hence he knew he must.

He swung the heavy wooden door open. Light flooded the center of the space. The many cracks in the walls illuminated the remainder of the interior. His mind raced to exactly how he'd repair the barn. He desperately wished for his grandfather, Finnean Munro, to see it once more as it had been, as it ought to always be, exactly as his grandfather had built it. To have it stand in this wretched state ate at his innards. If only his brother had lived.

He looked about him determined to avoid falling into that rabbit hole. He was not here to contemplate his situation in life. Pastor West had summoned him here for—what? He had not the foggiest idea.

"Cole?" a voice croaked from the darkest corner.

"Aye." He squinted, but the person remained cloaked in shadows. "To whom do I speak? Show yourself."

The dark figure emerged directly before him. And the moment light hit the man's face, it stole his breath. "Everett?"

"The one and only."

"But, how?" His body froze and his mind raced. "You're dead."

His brother chuckled. "I assure you, I am very much alive."

"I need to sit." He ambled to a bale of hay. "I must be running a high fever."

"I scarcely believed Pastor West when he told me you thought I had died, but I suppose 'tis true. You actually believed me dead?" Cole reached up and pinched his brother. "La! You need not apply a physical reprimand."

"'Tis not one. I only wished to ascertain if you truly were a living being."

"Once more, I assure you, I very much am. So you may refrain from causing me any further injury."

"Sorry. Wait, I am not. I thought you had died. Where have you been? Do you know how much I have grieved you? Do mother and father know you're alive? We must go at once to tell them." He sprang to his feet.

"Wait." He grabbed his arm. "Allow me to explain before you run out of here like a cat on fire." He grunted, but sat. "You mustn't tell anyone you've seen me."

"But—" His mind exploded with their future. The ranch would once more belong to his older brother. Everett would now court Jamilyn. He'd step away from it all. But the relief of knowing his brother had lived must console him. Grief and guilt melted away.

"Don't fret. Mother and father know I'm alive. As do, grandmother and grandfather. And Pastor West. But you must be the last one to ever know. My identity must be kept secret."

"You're a spy," he blurted.

His brother dipped his chin. "Just as dad had been. But my mission requires me to be someone else, hence I had to disappear. I never thought you'd ever have thought I had died."

"We were in a horse race and you disappeared. I thought you had fallen off a cliff or been killed by a wild animal."

"I know that mountain like the back of my hand. A wild animal? Have we not met before?" his six foot two, brawny brother bellowed. "And besides, I told you I had to leave."

Anger flared. "You did no such thing."

"Perhaps not in exact words, since I had been sworn to secrecy. But I did indeed indicate as much with several obvious hints." His mind flew back to that calamitous day. He did in fact remember his brother had spoken as if he knew his demise was eminent. "Apparently though, I failed to convey the particulars into that hard head of yours." He grimaced, causing his brother much laughter. "You must indeed possess one thick skull, for I've become aware of the fact that you failed to understand my other message to you on that day, as well."

"Which was?"

"You won the competition, Cole. You were supposed to court Jamilyn. You've been enamored with her since you first met her. I believed you required a push, and hence I issued you one before I left. And you most certainly ought to trust me in this matter, for I'd never lose such a race to you if I had actually competed." Everett ruffled his hair until he swatted his bear claw away.

"But I thought you had died. I'd never gain from your loss. And now, if

I hadn't just lived through so much regret and learned my lesson, I'd say we ought to redo the competition."

"There is no need. I do not love Jamilyn. I never have. I only concocted the competition to push you toward your heart's desire."

"I cannot believe any of this. I am most relieved and happy you're alive. And yet, my entire life has just changed in a matter of minutes."

Everett sat beside him with an enormous grin. "Aye, you are free to court her. And I do indeed wish you to inherit the ranch. I harbor no desire toward it. I made my wishes known the moment I chose this life of espionage."

"And you're happy?"

"I am. Father loved this life before he met mother, and I suppose like father, like son, I do, as well. Whereas you followed after dad once he had married and settled at the ranch. You have that part of him."

"And you shall remain safe?"

"God-willing."

"A day shall not pass where I shan't pray for you. And I do hope one day you return, and as father did, settle here. I have missed you dearly." His brother hugged him tight, and the weight of his burdens disappeared.

"Perhaps one day God shall favor me with a woman as wonderful as Mother, but until then, I must away and fulfil my duty."

"Are you not staying for Christmas?"

"I cannot. However, I shall sneak in a word with everyone at home before I go. And I promise I shall sneak back from time to time. But, next time I come, I had better hear the ranch is thriving under your leadership, and you've wed the love of your life."

"You know not what I have suffered. Hence, now that I have your blessing, I shan't waste another moment."

*　　*　　*

Jamilyn had never spent such an extensive length of time in dressing. However, she knew exactly why she moved as a sloth this day. Although

she did indeed wish to celebrate
Christmas Eve at church, her lack of
desire to be in the presence of Cole
overshadowed her usual holiday
merriment. She knew not how to behave
or what to say to him.

But perhaps they shan't even
greet one another, or speak as
friends. He had loved her, of that she
was sure. But he most certainly did
not love her now. And that contention
must part them, especially given the
fact that she did indeed love him.

On the outside it appeared as if
her situation with Lachlan had
repeated itself. She was in love with
someone who didn't love her. But her
situation with Cole was entirely
different. Her feelings for him made
her realize how superficial her
feelings for Lachlan had been. She had
been enamored with the idea of
Lachlan, not him. But Cole, she loved
him, inside and out. And as such,
she'd do anything to assure his
happiness and well-being.

Hence, she must put aside her
hopes of marriage, concentrate on
easing his mind in regards to his

confession, and then hopefully, they could remain friends. At least this way, she'd secure him as a friend for life.

She inhaled one final deep breath for encouragement, then strode to the church. Her plan involved arriving early, before the other parishioners, and inconspicuously seating herself, to avoid any uncomfortable encounters.

As she hurried toward the front door of the church, she slowed her steps somewhat, not one person roamed about. She had accomplished her task of arriving early. Her pa would be pleased, a most welcome subsequent benefit.

She scampered up the stairs. Her ankle no longer hurt, and she thanked God for that. Soon, she'd be seated in the warmth of the church. She reached for the door handle. The door swung toward her. She pulled back. "Merry Christmas, Cole," she sputtered, as she attempted to compose herself.

"Merry Christmas. May I speak with you privately?" he rushed his words. "'Tis early enough I think before others shall arrive." She nodded. "I've just spoken with your pa, he's within, so perhaps we could take a turn about the churchyard?"

"I believe the children have worn a path we may follow. It meanders into the woods."

"Splendid." They fell into step. "I arrived early with the express hope of finding you here so we could speak alone."

She stopped. "Cole, we need not be uncomfortable with one another. We're friends. And if the decision were mine, I'd declare we remain friends forever, regardless of—anything."

"I'm glad to hear you say as much. I agree whole heartedly." Her heart sank and elevated at the same time. She did not wish to be merely friends with him. And yet, she supposed it better than the alternative of losing him completely.

She turned and continued to walk. "Are your Christmas preparations finished?" she changed the subject entirely.

"Aye. And you?"

She nodded. "My pa is as excited as I remember being as a child. He's immensely happy I'm home, as I'm sure your family is, as well."

"They are. And they do not know it yet, but I am to give them the gift they most wish for this Christmas."

"Pray tell, what are you to surprise them with?"

"I shall tell them I do indeed wish to inherit the ranch."

She squealed, "Oh, Cole. I am so happy for you. For all of you."

He dipped his chin. "'Tis your father we must thank. He showed me something this Christmas that changed my mind."

"My pa?"

"Aye. And you, as well. You've helped me more than you know, for I have yet to thank you."

"You need not."

"But I do. You attempted to open my eyes to the life before me, and I wish you to know how dearly I appreciate your effort."

"'Twas not easy, I assure you. Apologizing." She shuddered. "I shan't do another naughty deed in my life, if

not just to avoid having to issue
apologies," she teased.

He laughed. "I know your heart.
You are no longer capable."

"I hope you're correct. And I
shan't even miss my gift from Lachlan
this Christmas."

His eyebrow raised. "Lachlan
presented you with gifts on Christmas?
I knew not anything of this."

"Every year after my mother left
us, I would find a gift under the
church Christmas tree addressed to me
with the inscription, Mr. M, and a
wish for me to enjoy a blessed
holiday. 'Tis another reason I
believed Lachlan in love with me."

"I understand your confusion even
more clearly now. Surely any man who
would present you with a gift year
after year must be in love with you,
would he not?"

"I believed so, but alas, some
men do these kind, considerate things
out of the goodness of their hearts I
suppose."

"I suppose. But I know not of any
men that match such a description."

"I fail to understand your meaning. You cannot seriously believe now that Lachlan loved me?"

He shook his head. Then reached into his pocket and pulled out a neatly wrapped present and handed it to her.

"But I have no gift for you," she mumbled.

"The only gift from you I desire is that you accept this present and read my note."

She hesitated, then flipped open the little card to read it aloud. Her eyes focused on the last line, and there she saw the same *Mr. M.* Her eyes snapped up to his. "Mr. M? You're Mr. M?"

"Mr. Munro." He dipped his chin. "I apologize, I could never bring myself to write my full name and reveal the gifts were from me."

"I thanked Lachlan every year for a gift that had actually come from you? He must have thought me insane."

"I doubt that. He must have assumed you were thanking him for some other kindness he had bestowed."

"I suppose." She laughed. Then, grew serious. "All those years though?"

He leaned in closer to her. "All those years, and all the years yet to come. I love you, Jamilyn. I have always loved you, and I shall love you forevermore."

Her mind failed to understand that which her heart knew. "But, I thought—your brother—you declared—"

He took her hand. "I have more to apologize for. I never ought to have allowed my situation with my brother to have come between us. Nothing shall ever keep me from you again." Worry etched his face. "Unless of course you do not feel the same."

Her heart leapt. "God has answered all my prayers, and more."

A grin slowly crept onto his face as understanding took hold.

"I love you, as well, Cole."

"Open your gift."

Her eyes darted down upon it. She had thought they'd kiss, or at least hug? "I don't need a gift, Cole. I have you. There is not any other gift that shall ever compare to you."

"Please, for me. Open it."

"Fine." She untied the ribbon and unfolded the paper. Then, she opened the box.

As she cried with delight, he took her hand and lowered himself onto one knee. "Jamilyn, please do me the honor of becoming my wife?" He took the ring from the box and held it up to her.

She nodded, a hand over her mouth to stop herself from either weeping or screaming, she knew not which. Her emotions flooded her. Pure joy, love, gratitude, and excitement radiated from her, shrouding her in a peace she had never felt. She was home to stay. This is where she belonged. Where she was loved. This man was her past, present, and future.

He slipped the gold ring on her finger. She stared at it as he stood. "Thank you for making me the happiest of men."

"'Tis I who ought to thank you. You rescued me from myself, and now, I am the happiest of women." She looked up into his sweet, caring eyes as they inched closer to her. When their lips touched she melted into him.

*   *   *

"I wish not to ever let you go, but I fear the other parishioners may begin to arrive soon." He kissed the top of her head, before allowing space between them.

"I suppose we ought to be sensible," she teased. "We have walked farther than I thought."

"Aye, but this bit of forest has sheltered us from the weather."

"And offered much needed privacy." Her cheeks flamed pink. He kissed her hand. But did not let it go as they walked back to the church.

"My pa shall be over the moon. Me to marry, and remain here."

"And raise a family."

"Me, a mother."

"Aye, and you shall be a wonderful mother. Our children shall be most fortunate."

"With you as their father I dare say they shall. And my pa, a grandfather. Oh, to bring him such happiness, and on Christmas."

"Aye, he could hardly contain his delight when I asked him for your hand."

Her head jerked toward him. "You did? When?"

"Before I bumped into you at the church door."

"You were inside asking my pa for my hand whilst I walked to church?"

He nodded. "I love you. And now that I've declared my love and know that you love me, I don't ever wish to be parted from you again."

She squeezed his hand. "My sentiments exactly."

They rounded the corner of the church and an uproar greeted them. There before them stood all their loved ones. "I could not help myself—" her pa shouted above the cheering as he hastened to them and embraced them both "—I mentioned the wondrous news to everyone I encountered."

"Which is the entire town, pa?"

"Aye." He laughed. "Now come and receive every blessed felicitation. I shall delay our service." He turned them toward the crowd and they cheered anew.

One by one every one of their family and friends offered their warmest wishes from the eldest members of their clan, Finnean and Cait, Logan and Sheena, and Angus and Nessia, to his cousins, Lachlan and Fiona, and, Blair and Penelope.

"I am most privileged to become a member of such a truly incredible family," she told him after everyone had entered the church and they stood alone in the fresh falling snow.

"We are the fortunate ones to have you join our family." He kissed her. Happiness and contentment coursed through his veins. He had wished for her to be his bride for so many years, and now 'twould finally happen. *Thank You, God.* "Have you considered when you may officially join our family, and become my bride?"

She smiled. "We are much changed, and I believe we ought not to bring any part of our old selves into the new year. We ought to usher in the new year as our new selves, begin anew, together."

"As much as I despise waiting even one more day, I concur that New Year's Eve shall be the perfect time to mark our new life together. And I cannot wait for our future to begin."

"I could not agree more. And I'm certain my father shall be only too happy to officiate. Now, let us go in before we miss the service. We have much to thank God for."

"Aye. But I dare say, after I've waited all these years, He shan't begrudge me—"

"One more kiss? I believe we are already of one mind." They laughed until their lips joined them as one.

Please Enjoy the other books in the

HIGHLAND HEARTS IN THE AMERICAS

Series

Book 1
CAPTURED HEARTS
He captured her homestead
She captured his heart
Highland Hearts
in the
Americas
1
An Inspirational Historical Romance Novel by Award Winning Author
Eva Maria Hamilton

On separate sides of the War of
1812, Lachlan McAllister and
Fiona Robertson are reunited.
But will their old feelings be
rekindled in time to save
Lachlan's life and lead them to
a future together?

With guest appearances from
beloved Highland Hearts
characters; Captured Hearts
begins a new series: Hearts in
the Americas, starring the
grandchildren of the couples
from Highland Hearts.

CAPTURED HEARTS
He captured her homestead
She captured his heart
Highland Hearts
in the
Americas
1
An Inspirational Historical Romance Novel by Award Winning Author
Eva Maria Hamilton

Book 2
GUARDED HEARTS
There are secrets
And then there are secrets that kill
Highland Hearts
in the
Americas
2
An Inspirational Historical Romance Novel by Award Winning Author
Eva Maria Hamilton

On a secret mission, Penelope
Sherwood is in enemy territory
in the Mohawk Valley of the
United States during the War of
1812. She's willing to risk
death to fulfill her late
father's dying request, but she
never expected to risk her
heart.

Meeting Blair McAllister was not
part of the plan. If he found
out her secret she could be
killed.

But what secret is he hiding?

GUARDED HEARTS
There are secrets
And then there are secrets that kill
Highland Hearts
in the
Americas
2
An Inspirational Historical Romance Novel by Award Winning Author
Eva Maria Hamilton

Dear Reader,

I hope you enjoyed Rescued Hearts!

It was fun to bring back all the Highland Hearts in the Americas' characters and finally have them all together, and of course at peace with one other, and themselves.

Jamilyn and Cole had to overcome deep regret and self-forgiveness, something that is not an easy task. But such is God's Grace. And I truly hope you know it.

I pray you also always know love and have the support of wonderful people in your life.

If you liked Jamilyn and Cole's story, please leave a review, they mean the world to me.

And please also connect with me.

I look forward to meeting you
and staying in touch!

Sincerely,

Eva Maria Hamilton

About the Author

Eva Maria Hamilton spent years studying people from all different areas of academia and brings that understanding of the human condition into each of her written pieces. An advocate for lifelong learning, Eva Maria Hamilton studied in both Canada and the United States, earning a diploma in Human Resources Management, a Bachelor of Arts degree in Psychology, an Honours Bachelor of Arts Degree in History, and a Master of Science in Education. She homeschooled her oldest daughter who is now in university, and still homeschools her youngest daughter, along with their two collies, while acting as Co-CEO in her Co-founded business, TestLauncher.

Eva Maria Hamilton is the author of Highland Hearts, a Love Inspired Historical novel published by Harlequin. Her novel, Highland Hearts:

- **Won 2nd Place in the Heart of Excellence, Reader's Choice Contest - Historical Romance Category**

- **Won 2nd Place in the Heart of Excellence, Reader's Choice Contest - Inspirational/Traditional Romance Category**

- Was an **Inspirational Series Finalist in the 2013 Gayle Wilson Award of Excellence**

Eva Maria Hamilton is also the owner of Lilac Lane Publishing, which has published a series of Jane Austen Colouring & Activity Books.

Her book, The Ultimate Collection of Jane Austen's Colouring and Activity Books: With More Than 240 Activities And Over 250 Illustrations from 1875-1906:

- Won the 2024 International Impact Book Awards.

Connect with the Author

To discover other books
Eva Maria Hamilton
has published, or soon will,
please visit her online:

EMAIL:
EvaMariaHamilton@gmail.com

FACEBOOK: Eva Maria Hamilton

FACEBOOK: Lilac Lane Publishing

X / TWITTER: @HamiltonEvaM

LINKEDIN: Eva Maria Hamilton

AMAZON.com: Amazon Author

AMAZON.ca: Amazon Author

LILAC LANE PUBLISHING:
www.LilacLanePublishing.com

WEBSITE:
www.EvaMariaHamilton.com

Highland Hearts

Scotland 1748

The Battle of Culloden is over, but one Highlander's fight has just begun — Logan McAllister survived years of indentured servitude in the Americas to reach this moment. Now he's returned to Scotland, ready to redeem the secret promise from Sheena Montgomery's father — that his years as a servant would earn him Sheena's hand in marriage. But when he arrives home, he learns that Sheena's father has died, his contract has been lost — and Sheena is engaged to another man.

"A good story that shows the lifestyles and prejudices that prevailed in 18th-century Scotland..."
Romantic Times

"Fascinating Scottish Romance...
Can't wait for more from this author."
5 Star Reviewer

"A great story about an interesting period...I look forward to reading more books by this new author."
5 Star Reviewer

"I found this to be a wonderful book...Highly recommend this book."
5 Star Reviewer

"An edge of your seat romance! Excellent! Loved it!"
5 Star Reviewer

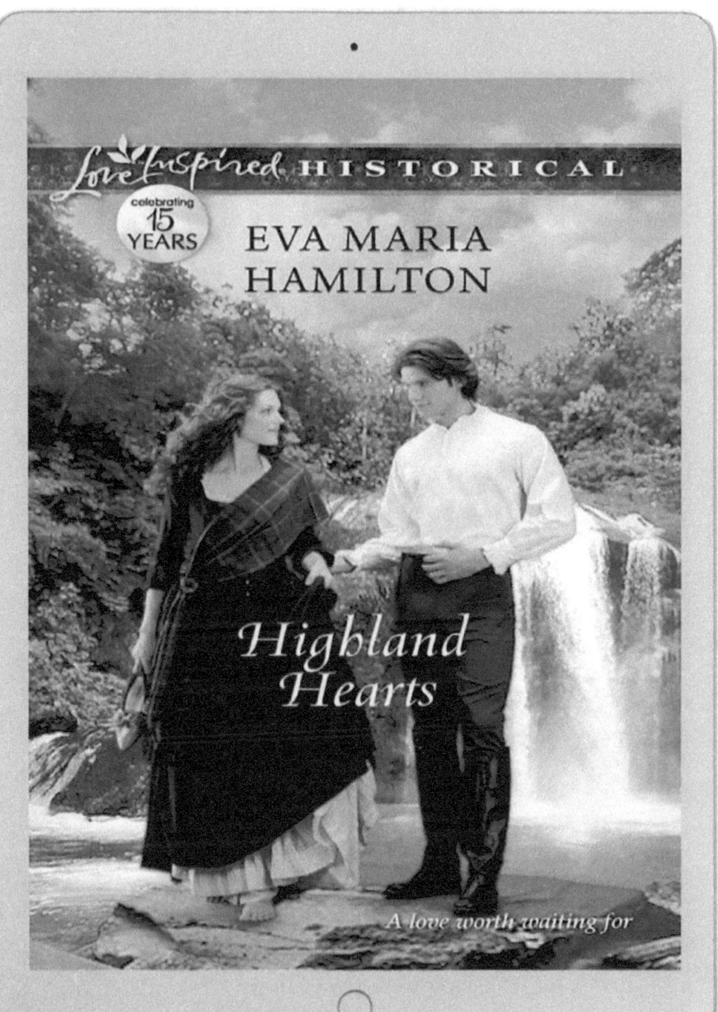

Love Inspired HISTORICAL
celebrating 15 YEARS
EVA MARIA HAMILTON
Highland Hearts
A love worth waiting for

Disinherited Love

Lily Chrisson and Lord Gavin Mackenzie hail from very different classes; a serious problem for those in love during Regency England. And yet, they're en route to secretly marry in Gretna Green. That is, until she discovers the truth. Torn apart, his determination wars with her principles, and family with even more secrets emerge in this redeeming short story.

**Step into the world
of Jane Austen!**

Immerse yourself in
colouring 40 illustrations
from the 1895 edition of
Pride and Prejudice.

Enjoy 40 activities, such
as Matching Characters to
Quotes, Search Words,
Anagrams, and more.

Have fun in the Regency
Era!

"...If you are a fan of Pride and Prejudice you will love this book. The illustrations are wonderful and the activities are engaging."
5 Star Reviewer

**Rated
5 Stars
on
Amazon**

★★★★★

Step into the world
of Jane Austen!

Immerse yourself in
colouring 40
illustrations from the
1896 edition of Sense
and Sensibility.

Enjoy 40 activities,
such as Matching
Characters to Quotes,
Search Words, Anagrams,
and more.

Have fun in the Regency
Era!

Rated
5 Stars
On
Amazon
★★★★★

Step into the world
of Jane Austen!

Immerse yourself in
colouring 40 illustrations
from the 1896 edition of
Emma.

Enjoy 40 activities, such
as Matching Characters to
Quotes, Search Words,
Anagrams, and more.

Have fun in the Regency
Era!

"*Beautifully presented...
Lovely as a gift.*"
Reviewer

Rated

5 Stars

on

Amazon

Step into the world
of Jane Austen!

Immerse yourself in
colouring 20 illustrations
from the 1897 edition of
Persuasion.

Enjoy 20 activities, such
as Matching Characters to
Quotes, Search Words,
Anagrams, and more.

Have fun in the Regency
Era!

*"Very educational...
Very beautiful."*

Reviewer

**Rated
5 Stars
on
Goodreads**

★★★★★

Step into the world of Jane Austen!

Immerse yourself in
colouring 40
illustrations from the
1897 edition of
Mansfield Park, plus 7
bonus illustrations
from the 1875 edition.

Enjoy 47 activities,
such as Matching
Characters to Quotes,
Search Words, Anagrams,
and more.

Have fun in the Regency
Era!

Rated
5 Stars
on
Amazon
★★★★★

Step into the world
of Jane Austen!

Immerse yourself in
colouring 20
illustrations from the
1897 edition of
Northanger Abbey.

Enjoy 20 activities,
such as Matching
Characters to Quotes,
Search Words, Anagrams,
and more.

Have fun in the Regency
Era!

Rated
5 Stars
on
Amazon
and
Goodreads
★★★★★

The Ultimate Collection
of Jane Austen's
Colouring & Activity Books

All
6 Books in 1
Plus More

Pride & Prejudice
Sense & Sensibility
Emma
Mansfield Park
Persuasion
Northanger Abbey

Plus Bonus Illustrations, and Activities From Her Other Writings:
Sandition, Lady Susan, The Watsons, Letters, and more.

By: Eva Maria Hamilton

With More Than 240 Activities
And Over 250 Illustrations from 1875-1906

The Ultimate Collection
of Jane Austen's
Colouring and Activity
Books, including:
Pride and Prejudice,
Sense and Sensibility,
Emma,
Mansfield Park,
Persuasion, and
Northanger Abbey.

Plus bonus
illustrations
and activities
from her other
writings:
Sandition,
Lady Susan,
The Watsons,
Letters,
and more.

With more than
240 activities
and over 250
illustrations
from 1875-1906!